MORANA

1 - BETH

She walked into the kitchen to pour herself a glass of red wine. It had been a typical day at the office making deals and making money. She was a successful investment banker with a very unique hobby. She undressed and slipped into her comfy clothes. She sipped her wine and got ready to check her inbox.

She had no unrealistic expectations of finding Mr. Right. She wasn't searching for the long stem roses and the white horse; in fact she had very different reasons for joining the site. She pulled up 123weddings.com. She typed the username and password for her profile. She was Morana. She used a fictitious profile picture, but it was still one that resembled her attractiveness. The likeness in beauty was so close, she knew there would be no issues when she met men in person. She described herself as an attractive thirty-something. Long dark hair, 5' 6", athletic, in great shape, 128 lbs, 32c, and curvy. She tried being as honest as possible with her description while avoiding anything that could actually identify her. She certainly didn't want to be identified.

With such an attractive profile picture, there was never a shortage of men eager to meet her. Tonight was no exception.
She had fourteen new potential future "husbands" in her inbox. As she typically did, she began the process of weeding through them. Not being heartless she simply replied with a no thank you to the honest guys who were searching for, and in obvious need of, a date. She could always weed them out. They looked like they were searching for anyone that would be willing to

go out with them. She felt sorry for them. They were probably the men who would actually respect a woman and were sincere in their attempts in finding a soulmate; however, these weren't the type of profiles she was searching for in her inbox. She was searching for a very specific type of men, and had no problem finding them.

Morana's real name was Beth, and Beth had met too many of these types of guys Morana was searching for. She had fallen victim to men who would say they were searching for that special someone, men who would come on strong until they got what they were looking for. Whether they were victorious in their search, or gave up, their profile was gone the next day and they were never heard from again. These guys were bad but they weren't who Morana was looking for.

Beth had met men who used the dating site as if it were a competition. These guys would act sincere while trying to meet as many women as possible in their search for "marriage". The problem was they had no intent of becoming a groom and no intent of entering into a monogamous relationship. These men were trying to date as many unsuspecting women as possible, all under false pretenses. A woman would meet one of these men, become involved, and develop feelings. They would begin seeing the possibility of a future only to find him on a date with someone else or catch him when he slipped up and called them by another's name. These guys were heartless, but they weren't the type of guys Morana was looking for.

Beth had met too many guys who were interested in sending revealing pictures of themselves or requesting revealing pictures of any willing girl. She felt confident most of these guys used fictitious pictures. These men would pour on the charm. If they were able to get a girl to send revealing or nude pictures of herself, all too many times they would end up on the internet alongside an e-mail to the girl and a website where the pictures could be seen. The girls on the receiving end of this type of guy felt so used and so embarrassed. This embarrassment was made worse when the email was sent to all the mutual friends they shared on the dating site. These women were so ashamed, but what recourse did they have? They typically removed their profile and, if they weren't already, became ever more wary of men. This often pushed them even further away from meeting someone they could care about and who would care about them. The men who did this were horrible, but these weren't the type of men Morana was looking for.

2 - JON

Morana was looking for a specific type of man. Beth had met this type of man, and had even fallen for this type of man. Beth met Jonathan Neal on a similar dating site. He was nice, polite, financially secure, and it didn't hurt that she found him GQ attractive when they met. He hadn't been deceptive on his profile about his looks or the fact that he was athletic and fit. As his profile described, he looked ready for a triathlon with the body to get him over the finish line. He was kind, compassionate, educated, and loved to travel; he even loved puppies. Jon was perfect.

Before she knew it, they were dating frequently. He had offices in New York and Florida. She soon found herself spending all her free time with him during his visits to his New York office. It made her feel even better when it was noticeable that the more time they spent together, the more meetings he seemed to have in New York. They shared similar interest in their careers and very similar interest in their relationship. She was a money manager and he owned a software company that made, among other things, financial software. They seemed to share the same goals: marriage, family and long vacations abroad (although maybe not in that order). She was successful with a talent for timing the market. He seemed to have founded a very successful, very profitable software company. In fact, he had mentioned he was in the initial stages of a buyout on one of their first dates. Everything seemed perfect. If only she had known how drastically this man would change her life, as well as the lives of so many men like him. He was the type of man Morana was looking for.

Their relationship was going well. They saw each other almost weekly, even shared the occasional weekend. She realized she missed the obvious signs when they spent all of their time together in New York. She had made one trip to Florida but only for a night. They stayed at a plush hotel near his office but traveled back to

New York early the following morning. She actually never made the connection; someone made it for her.

It was a Thursday night. She and Jon had recently come back from dinner and had just finished dessert in her bedroom before heading to the airport for his flight back to Florida. It seemed odd he left so late at night m; however, with his business in the middle of a buyout, she knew things could be hectic. In one of their many emails. Jon told her the two companies were having trouble reaching an agreement. With her experience in finance and understanding of takeovers, she had offered her help in any way possible. She had been taken off guard when he asked for financial backing in one email. When she responded asking if he'd been serious, he played it off and said her free advice was all the financial backing he needed. She jokingly said to bribe the board, then the conversation moved to a more sexual nature as it so often did. They discussed his next trip to New York and his desire to take her to dinner followed by one of their many bedroom desserts.

It had been over two months and she had all but forgotten about her dating site profile. It was sheer coincidence that she logged in that night. She was actually signing on to update her profile status to "in a relationship" and make a note on her profile about the perfect man she had met and how, for her, the site had been very successful. Before she made the changes she noticed an email in her inbox. It almost seemed ironic that the message had arrived just a few minutes earlier. She was weeding through and deleting the older emails she had responded to and those she knew she never would. When she noticed the email, she almost deleted it but was intrigued by the profile name. She had no way of knowing at the time but the person calling themselves "Life Changer" was going to be exactly that.

She opened the email which simply read: This Saturday, Four Points, Cocoa Beach at 2:00 pm. She didn't think much about it at first. She assume it was a random guy who wanted her to meet at a beach assuming she would find that romantic and make the trip. Again, she had almost hit the delete key but stopped. She just found the profile name too intriguing. Out of curiosity, she decided to go to Life Changer's page and read the profile. She became even more interested when she discovered there was nothing listed on the profile. No picture, no personal information, not even information on the type of person life changer was searching for.

She spent the remainder of the night thinking about the email until the notion finally hit her; it was Jon. Of course it was Jon. He was trying to surprise her and wanted her to come to Cocoa Beach for something special, something romantic nonetheless. That would explain why he had left early tonight, he needed to get back to be sure the Cocoa Beach surprise was perfect. She always pegged him for a romantic, but as she began to wonder what surprise he had planned, she couldn't help thinking he was about to blow past your run of the mill and stereotypical sweetheart. She called the airlines and booked her flight for first thing Saturday morning. She was excited and had trouble falling asleep, something that almost never happened. She had learned to put anxiety behind her in her years of following the markets. This was different, this was excitement. She couldn't wait. For just the briefest of seconds, she let herself think that maybe he was going to ask her to marry him.

The plane landed and she quickly made her way to Four Points Cocoa Beach. It was November, and she was excited to trade the cold temperatures of New York for a few days of mild Florida weather. On the way there, she found herself almost giddy. She wasn't use to feeling anything like this. She had been hurt several times in the past and had put a vault around her heart, a vault which apparently took Jon only a few short months to walk right through. He had already surprised her. He surprised her that in such a short time someone was able to renew feelings she hadn't felt for so long, even giddiness apparently.

She walked into the hotel and approached the front desk. As she gave her name she was told all the arrangements had been made for her. It appeared Jon had taken care of everything. She was given instructions as to a time and location. She went to her room, showered, and put on her best face. She dressed in a new Gucci outfit and headed to Cocoa Beach. She had two hours before she was supposed to go to the beach, so she became a tourist. She took a cab to Minuteman Causeway and decided to take a stroll. It didn't take long for her to start to question why she was here at this location. The beach and area were both nice, but Jon owned a lucrative software business. This place seemed a little below what she would have expected. No exclusive resorts, no members only clubs, and no romantic hideaways in sight. She made her way up A1AN across 2nd Avenue and decided to stop in The Pig and Whistle English Pub. She was a little turned around and asked for directions to her spot on the beach. The bartender told her she was within walking distance.

She headed down 2nd street and passed a tattoo shop on her way to the beach. She was growing more startled by the location and how it was filled with tourists and lacked high-end anything. She told herself maybe the location held some special meaning for Jon. Maybe he had saved a person from drowning when he was young. Maybe he owned a little restaurant or local pub, anything but the tattoo shop she hoped. She couldn't think of any reason why he would ask her to this beach, but as she approached the beach she saw a crowd and thought she saw Jon close to the water. They had never really talked about his family, and she thought perhaps this was where his family lived and he wanted them to meet her.

She headed towards the crowd and noticed how nicely Jon was dressed. He was barefoot and wearing khaki linen pants with a red linen long sleeve polo shirt. Beth was wearing a new slightly revealing beach outfit and was concerned she was not dressed appropriately for whatever he had set up for her. She had only met a few of Jon's colleagues and didn't recognize any of the people in the crowd. She noticed that there were several guys all dressed the same. They each had on linen pants identical to Jon's, and they were also wearing red linen long sleeve polo shirts. Surely Jon wasn't this presumptuous. So many thoughts raced through her mind in the matter of seconds. Would she say yes? How excited she became when she saw the guys dressed the same. Did she love this guy, did he love her? Would they get a puppy? She couldn't help laughing out loud when that thought popped into her head.

She stopped walking towards the beach once she saw Jon, but began to walk his way when she regained her composure. She was nearing the sand when she noticed there were several women wearing identical clothes as well. She hadn't really thought about it until just then, but if he were there to marry her, what would she do about bridesmaids? After all, he had groomsmen. She slipped off her Peche Platinum flip-flops with a quick chuckle. She couldn't help laughing at the irony that five percent of the costs of her crocodile flip flops going to groups working to prevent the extinction of primates. She placed her foot in the sand and was about to call out Jon's name when she noticed there was a woman wearing a dress that resembled the dresses worn by three other women. She stopped dead in her tracks as music began to play. Jon was standing less than a block away from her on the beach when she noticed the woman was carrying a bouquet of blue and white flowers and walking towards him.

She realized, as the woman approached, that there was a man standing between them. All at once she realized two things. First, she was at a beach wedding, which explained the flower bouquet. Second, and all too quickly, she wasn't the one getting married.

She watched the ceremony unfold. She wanted to leave or fight or hit or anything violent but instead she just sat there. slowly realizing that she had, once again, played the role of the fool. She had been used by another man. She made the mistake of giving her heart to someone who had not only broken it, but had shattered it with lies, betrayal, and humiliation. It hit her like a rock. Had Jon been Life Changer? Had he actually asked her here to witness this? Had he brought her to this beach, where families watch their kids play in the water? He had made all these arrangements? He had done all this?

She watched as long as she could. She watched for what seemed like an eternity before turning to walk away. She saw an attractive couple walking towards her; she used to be that couple. They were walking hand in hand, happy and smiling. They were in love, which made her realize she was in love. She was in love with this man that made her feel again, made her care again, and now made her broken again. She felt a feeling she hadn't felt in so long. A feeling she worked so hard to make herself immune to. She felt weak. She felt defeated. As the couple passed, she managed to hold her composure until the women passing asked if she was there to watch Jon and Sara renew their wedding vows. She felt gravity intensify and had to fight to keep from collapsing. She felt wounded in a way she never felt. In a moment, she recalled all her past heartbreaks--but none compared to this. With that one sentence, she was no longer defeated. She was no longer heartbroken; in fact, she was no longer broken at all. With that one sentence, she became filled with rage. Jon didn't know it, but he hadn't made Beth sad; instead, he had just brought Morana to life. And Morana was very angry.

3 - Anonymity

She went back into the swing of things surprisingly easily. She had not heard from Jon in almost two weeks, but was quite certain he was on his second honeymoon. She hadn't really thought of what she would say or how she was going to handle hearing from him. In fact, she hadn't really thought about him in a romantic, someone you care about, way. He had been on her mind, however. She had come back to New York and had decided another dating site might be better for her since her previous one held Beth's information, the information that could identify a person who was going to become completely different. There was no question; she was going to need a new profile to match her new life.

She purchased a new laptop, a laptop with the highest level of encrypted security. A laptop with WiFi so it could be used anywhere. She purchased a prepaid cellular phone from a street vendor, the type that offered internet usage. The computer whiz who worked at the coffee shop she frequented once told her he could tether any cell phone with an internet connection to a laptop and voila; it would be connected. He constantly talked about technical jargon which she almost never understood. One of the few things he said that she understood was how to scramble your ip address. He mentioned software that allowed you to surf the internet while being untraceable.

She had her new laptop. After spending two hundred and fifty dollars, and flirting with a coffee shop tech nerd, she knew how to anonymously connect to the internet anywhere she had her disposable cell phone. She had her new profile. She had her new identity. She had her new hobby.

4 - Lifechanger

Beth periodically checked her profile. When she returned from Florida, she had replied to Life Changer, but had gotten no response. She assumed Jon was Life Changer and he didn't have the courage to face her and had chosen this horrible way to end their relationship. She thought it was both cowardly and incredible brave. For all he knew, she could have arrived in Florida and gone right up to his wife and apprise her of their liaisons. She also wanted to see if Jon would contact her via his online profile. He hadn't for several weeks. She began to think he may have changed and become a faithful married man again, or was this word again giving him undue credit? Had he ever been a faithful married man? There was a message from him tonight, Her expectations were realized; he had attempted to contact her. She was surprised to find she felt no emotion. She was going through a renewal.

She opened the email and read his explanation of why he hadn't been in contact for so long. He had an unexpected meeting surrounding the buyout and had to leave town. He was sorry he couldn't call, but the information wasn't public and any slip could cost his company millions of dollars. He had no choice but to keep his trip secret from all of his personal and intimate friends. She read the email with the same feeling one would have reading the nutritional content of rice. She did get a kick out of the fact that he said 'intimate' in the same sentence he used the plural of friends. She barely finished the email before she was typing her response.

She sent a simple reply telling Jon she was sorry but would be busy with work and she felt they shouldn't see each other anymore. She explained she was going to delete his profile from her allowable friends on the dating site and that she would appreciate it if he wouldn't contact her again. She would be in touch if her feelings changed, but that she just wasn't ready to continue their relationship and had actually been dating several other guys. She was sorry and wished him well.

She felt comfortable he wouldn't contact her since he was married, and married men were usually all too happy to accept a free out. Out of an adulterous relationship they had gotten away with, especially when it was all too apparent they had no intentions of having anything other than a naughty little affair. She didn't hear back from Jon over the next several days and assumed he was no longer a part of her life. At the time, she didn't realize how much a part of her life he had unwillingly become.

5 - DATES

She sat in front of her computer screen, logging into Morana's account, and began thinking. She found herself thinking back to how nervous she had been on her first "date". She recalled how she had almost backed out, thought she wouldn't be able to go through with it. She thought about how easy she found it to be once she actually began and how she felt no guilt after she finished. She remembered how her attitude and actions changed at work the week following her first date. She remembered how her colleagues had noticed no change in her personality. How Morana had been able to remain White Collar Beth. She remembered how easy it was, and how natural it felt, to become a different person. She remembered that Morana had come to life the second she was asked if she was there for Jon's wedding vow renewals.

She accepted requests from men who said they read her profile and felt they shared common interests. She accepted requests from men who said they found her attractive and wanted to get to know her. She accepted requests from men who said they were just out of relationships and were looking for someone they could be friends with first. Her personal favorite were those men who proclaimed to be heartbroken and afraid they would never be able to love again. Morana had seen so many ways men attempted to use and manipulate women through the profiles while keeping their real lives hidden.

She accepted most requests, but very few made it through her screening process. She quickly eliminated those that didn't meet her qualifications. If they were nice and seemed sincere, she would usually say she already met someone. If they were brash or seemed to be looking for a one night stand or something dirty, like conversation or pictures, she would rudely tell them they weren't good enough for her. It was when they seemed too good to be true or someone they obviously weren't that she would accept their request and begin conversations. She would usually talk with them for a while to see if they'd ask to meet; they always did.

She would screen a guy who seemed to fit the right profile, accept a date, and even act interested. It didn't take long for her to realize how petty men were. With her looks, she was able to easily control relationships almost immediately. She was able to accomplish this without her "dates" realizing it. She would act as if she wanted a boyfriend and tell the man what a great catch he was. She would tell him how handsome and funny he was, and of course mentions how she thought he would be great in bed. With her puppy dog eyes and her timid demeanor, they would feel they had found the perfect candidate; in other words, the perfect target. She quickly realized men were so easy, especially once the bedroom conversation started. They never realized by that time Morana was in control and they were the target.

She knew that for the right men, those that met her qualifications, she had every intention of spending time with them in the bedroom. What the men didn't realize was the time they spent in the bedroom with Morana would be in no way like their expectations.

She intentionally never let the men

know where she lived. She would always insist on meeting them in public places, places nowhere near her apartment. In fact she created a fictitious residence, a fictitious job, a fictitious everything. There was no Beth when she met men.

She once met a guy who asked if she was willing to travel. He said he felt he had home field advantage if she came to see him. When he said that she thought to herself how funny, but predictable, a man's mind worked. She thought it would be easier to tell if they met her qualifications if she traveled to them. If she traveled to their house, and it seemed to be a bachelor's pad, she could be sure there was never a second visit.

Her standard was to tell the man how nice he was, but that she had met another person and was going to delete her profile. She was looking for men who said they were on business and needed to meet at a hotel, or constantly traveled and had to come to her. Men always had reasons why she couldn't come to their home They were moving, remodeling, or any of the countless other reasons. She met one man who said he had won the lottery and was staying at a hotel while his new house was being built. She remembered how fun he was.

Her name was Morana to these men but her life was different each time. Nothing was real; she wanted no trace back to Beth or the real world. Morana met many men and would occasionally find a guy who touched her or almost give her faith in men again, but it inevitably went back to Jon. There was always a Jon that renewed her hatred and justification for her hobby. Always a Jon. These were the type of men she was looking for.

She recalled the first "date" that met her qualifications. He fell into the heartbroken and never able to love again category. He met her qualifications from the onset of their very short lived relationship. The fact that he met these qualifications probably aided in how easy she found it was to become Morana. She surprised herself at how easy it was to end their "relationship" as she so quickly did after realizing he was her type.

She came home from work and logged into her account, which she now did nightly. She noticed a request from "SadBrian" in her inbox and accepted it. He said he was Brian, a 35 year old, who had recently been hurt, but hoped to find someone to help mend his broken heart. She was suspicious from the first email. She replied that she was sorry he had such a bad experience and that she would love to talk to him and maybe even meet at some point. She immediately had him. He went right to saying he "may be able to meet at some point". She directed the conversation for the balance of the night. In no time, he was explaining how he traveled a lot with work. He lived in South Carolina, but traveled to New York frequently. She found it amusing how almost every man she communicated with traveled to New York for work, and frequently.

Their conversations lasted almost a week before he told her he was headed to New York for work and would love to meet her. Something told her he was just her type, so she agreed. She offered to pick him up at the airport. He said he was from South Carolina so she found it odd he was flying in from Georgia. He said he was traveling for work. Of course, she said.

6 - GOODBYE BETH

Donning an auburn wig, glasses, heavy coat and scarf, she used her newly acquired alias to rent a small apartment across the Queensboro Bridge. Her glasses were the basic brown framed reading glasses and the coat was plain, grey, and heavy enough to mask her physique. She had all three of the coats buttons done so nothing was visible above her knees. She was very impressed with how realistic the wig looked. She wanted to be a blond, but it wouldn't have been smart; she didn't want to be remembered for having blond hair. Besides, it wouldn't have fit her forgettable motif. How many New Yorkers have natural blond hair? The scarf was very bland and boring. Just for good measure, she purchased green contacts to cover her blue eyes and doused herself in make-up, something she rarely wore. She felt comfortable that she had covered her black hair, blue eyes, great complexion, and fit body. She had become your average anybody, your average nobody.

She rented an apartment that looked as if it fit her made up receptionist job and, more importantly, she felt it was far enough away from Beth's Upper West Side apartment. She found that most men had little to no interest in hearing about her mundane life as a receptionist. Her new apartment was far enough away from her Manhattan penthouse and boring enough to not be the topic of discussion. She found that men wanted to talk about, and hear about, themselves. She would nonchalantly move the conversation in that direction when questions were asked that required any detailed answer about her personal life. She found that, by learning from men, she could be quite the liar.

It was late afternoon on Friday when she met Brian, from South Carolina or Georgia, or wherever he was from, at the airport. It was obvious that his broken heart had mended in the short time they had been talking. He was overly affectionate when they met and couldn't wait to get back to her place. He said he needed to wash the flight off him before dinner. When he planned his trip, he told her he would be staying for three days but he wasted no time in letting her know his plans had changed, he was only going to be in town for the night. He excused himself, said he would be right back, and said he had to make a call. She felt confident she had met her type.

They made it back to her apartment and he was barely in the door when he mentioned for the second time he needed to wash the travel off. She pointed him to the bathroom and waited until she was sure he was in the shower before she began looking through his clothes. She found his wallet and found a picture. The picture was of him beside a woman that certainly appeared to be his beautiful wife. She continued to look through his pants and found his wedding ring inside his front pocket. She knew then that he was exactly the type she was looking for. He was the type Morana was looking for and she had found him.

7 - BRIAN

Brian walked out of the bathroom and, in such a predictable manner, suggested they skip dinner. Lacking any originality, he asked if she wanted to open a bottle of wine and just get to know each other. She said that sounded like a great idea and moved closer to him. While he was in the shower, she had intentionally changed into a low cut, thin shirt, which revealed very noticeable very intentional cleavage. Brian, being a guy, didn't even notice her right hand indiscriminately concealed behind her back. He was busy thinking about how it had only taken a little over week to go from sending emails to being in her apartment. He was thinking about how easy it had been to get her to stay in and drink wine. She knew he was thinking how much easier it would be for him if she had a few glasses of wine. He was so conceited. He was so sure, and so wrong, about what he knew was going to happen. She was almost in front of him before he noticed she was holding something in her left hand.

By the time he realized it was there, she was already holding her left hand close to his face asking him to tell her about the picture. It took a second, but as he looked at the picture of his wife, he realized she was also wearing his wedding ring on her left thumb. He had a blank look on his face and was trying desperately to think of an answer. Before he could say his first word, he noticed her right hand come from behind her back. Before he had a chance to focus, it was too late. She had put the stun baton to his genitals, that's the last thing he remembered. He was incapacitated when she removed the baton; all he could do was breathe in the chloroform as she placed the cloth over his face.

Fortunately for her, though quite unfortunately for Brian, he had over compensated on his profile. He was 3 inches shorter than the 5' 11" he said he was. He described himself as muscular but wasn't. He was actually skinny. Morana was fit and athletic and was able to move him with little effort. He hadn't noticed when he placed his overnight bag on the bed it was on rollers.

8 - INVESTMENT PROPERTY

She had purposely rented the end apartment on the last floor of her 8 story building. No building close to hers was high enough to see into her windows. It was sheer luck that the apartment next to hers wasn't occupied. What were the odds of two apartments in New York not rented? She couldn't help thinking how it had to be more than coincidental both were empty and how it was an omen for any man who visited her "home". The layout was perfect; the apartment opened into a small hallway with the bedroom and bathroom on the right. There was a wall dividing the bedroom and the kitchen, which was in the right corner of the apartment. The kitchens were in the corners of the building and had brick walls on both sides. It opened into the den on the left corner of the apartment. The only windows were in the bedroom and the den. Only the entrance into the kitchen was visible by the den window. That left the kitchen as a perfect place for her rolling bed.

9 - FIRST DATES

He woke up and the soreness from the baton jolted him from his groggy haze. It took several minutes for him to realize where he was. He started to gain a little clarity and realized he was naked. He saw Morana. She walked to the right side of the bed he was strapped to and looked down at him. He was trying to speak when she began talking to him. She was short and precise with her statements. She had a ball pin hammer in her hand and placed it on his knee cap. She said if he made any noise, she would start with his left knee cap before moving to his right. She asked if he understood and he replied yes with a nod. She was holding the picture of his wife in her hand and asked him to tell her who the person was. She wanted him to use her name so he had to acknowledge he was hurting a real person. He said his wife's name was Kim.

He noticed a mirror on the ceiling, which allowed him to see how he was strapped to a bed. He could also see the bed was on a plastic tarp, which covered the floor, and a tray that seemed to be full of items he couldn't make out. The bed wheels had been locked in place. He had ratchet straps wrapped twice tightly around each foot then secured to the bed frame on each side. He had the same tying his hands. He noticed a device attached to a makeshift headboard that had two metal arms sticking out, one on each side of his head. He realized there were sharp metal ice pick looking points sticking out from each arm. The tip of each metal point was less than an inch from his orbital socket. He rolled his head slightly to his right and could see the tip. He realized if he moved his head an inch in either direction the tip of the metal point would pierce his eye. He had a ratchet strap wrapped twice around his chest under his armpits. The strap was wrapped underneath the bed with the ratchet locked on each side of the frame. He was essentially immobile with the exception of his head. He quickly realized moving it would be unbearably painful, not to mention permanently detrimental.

She had made so many arrangements prior to meeting her first "date". She was untraceable, thanks to the tech nerd and software in her computer and tethered cell phone. She avoided Wi-Fi when in her apartment. Makeup and wig intact, she made frequent trips to the Brooklyn Public Library when she needed to use the internet for any search that might appear suspicious. She had quickly discovered how easy it was to buy secure technology on the internet.

Morana ask if he wanted to say anything before she began. As he tried to ask what "began" meant, she shoved a cloth in his mouth. She had a piece of torn duct tape on the headboard, which she placed over his mouth. She picked up a cattle prod he hadn't noticed sitting on the bed beside him. She slowly moved it down his stomach, which quickly reminded him of the fact he was completely undressed. She stopped at his testicles and applied what would be the first of several shocks.

To no avail, he tried to scream. Even if he didn't have a cloth shoved in his mouth covered by duct tape, it was unlikely he would be heard. She explained he was on the top floor and the end apartment. Leaning close to his right ear, she whispered there was an empty apartment next to hers and the brick on both sides muffled the kitchen walls. He had no way of knowing it but any attempt to be heard or discovered was pointless. Knowing the answer, she asked if his wife knew about his date site profile and if anyone knew about his profile or his attempts at adultery. They both knew the answer. She wanted him to be afraid, to be terrified, and he was. She could see the fear in his eyes and the increasing heartbeat in his chest. She explained that Morana was a made up person with no contact information other than a made up email on an untraceable computer. Morana, the unidentifiable corrector of adulterous wrongs, was about to make her first "broken hearted" victim pay for his actions.

10 - APOLOGIES

He wanted to say he was sorry and that he hadn't meant to hurt anyone. He wanted to say he loved his family and he would never cheat on his wife again. He wanted to say anything, but quickly realized it was too late for apologies or confessions. Had he been able to speak, it would have only intensified the rage inside Morana. Brian had become Jon. She picked the ball pin hammer up and struck his right knee cap. She didn't want to shatter his knee cap, so she hit only hard enough to crack it. She could tell the hit had caused the desired effect by Brian's reaction. Not sure if it was shattered or even cracked, she decided to hit the left knee. She struck this knee with enough force to, at a minimum, shatter the cap. She could tell that this hit caused far more damage than the previous.

She left the room for a few minutes and let Brian lay there feeling the pain from both hits. She was surprised at his ability to take the pain without moving his head to either side. She thought for sure he would blind himself before they even got started. She was happy he hadn't. She walked back into the room holding a small kit. He couldn't make out what was in the kit initially but looking into the mirror he could see there we several objects.

She removed a small surgical knife and leaned in towards him. With her lips a few inches away from his ear, she whispered a chilling reminder that there was a steel tip on each side of his eyes. She suggested that he hold very still and, with a devious look, she leaned over him and with a pause said…"there will be tears".

In one hand, she held a pair of rubber tipped ring opening pliers, which she used to slowly lift his left eyelid by the lashes. Brian was sweating and trying to scream, but the rag and duct tape muted all sound. Using the pliers to gently pull it away from his eye, she took the surgical knife and made an incision down the middle of his left eye lid. He could fill the blood pour into his eye as he felt the pain from the cut. She took a small rag and placed in over his eye to absorb the blood. She told him this next cut may be a little more painful, but that surely he knew about pain; after all he was able to hurt his family with ease. Using his eyelashes, she lifted his right eyelid with the pliers. She took the surgical knife and sliced his right eyelid off. Again, he felt both the pain and the blood. He felt as if he was going to pass out from the pain radiating from both his knees and eye. She told him how proud she was he had managed to keep his head still. She took a second rag and placed it over his right eye.

She sat there for a few minutes and let the rags absorb the blood before removing them. She poured rubbing alcohol into his eyes and wiped them clean. She placed another clean rag on each eye. She stood up and walked over to the kit she had placed on a small table beside the bed. In a calm voice, she told Brian that the bleeding was bad but not to worry she was going to help it stop. He couldn't see, but he could hear her moving beside him. She removed a battery operated soldering iron from her kit. While the iron was heating, she removed the rags from each eye. She wiped the blood from one eye and he was able to see she had something in her hand. She took the iron and placed it on the cut down the middle of the eyelid he had left; the bleeding stopped. She walked over to his right side and, with a new rag, wiped the blood clean. She wanted him to see the iron coming towards his eye, and he did. She reminded him to be very still as she placed the hot tip on near his eye. She stopped short of his eyeball and told him not to worry; she would never blind him in both eyes; that would mean he wouldn't enjoy the rest of their date with the same intensity. "You did hope tonight would be intense, right?", she asked him. She sat in a chair at the foot of the bed waiting for the bleeding to stop, periodically getting up to wipe his eye with rubbing alcohol.

She sat quietly for a few minutes. She wanted to be sure Brian didn't pass out. Once she was sure he was conscious, she asked if he was in any pain. He wanted to scream yes, but all he could do was slowly move his head up and down. She asked if he could appreciate the pain he was inflicting in the lives of those he hurt. As he tried to nod yes, she answered for him. She told him if she stopped, his pain would only last a short period of time, but the pain he inflicted on others would last a lifetime. She asked if he thought that was fair to them. She stood up and walked to him. She placed her hand on his knee and squeezed. She said she didn't think it was fair either.

As he was lying there in almost unbearable pain, she left the room and went to her laptop. She logged into Morana's account and searched her inbox. She knew that by reading the messages from the "dates" she had planned for the future that she would soon become more enraged.

Unfortunately for Brian, there were plenty of men.

She read through a few of the new messages in her inbox and, out loud, re-read several of the ones she had marked as potential new dates. There were several from men who seemed lonely or horny or simply too shy to meet a women through any other avenue. There was one in particular, however, that sparked her interest. She opened a new online date invite from username "HungDavid". Right away, she knew she didn't like him and this was bad news for Brian. She read through the text from "HungDavid" and became furious. There was only one line of text and it read "married and looking for a friends with benefits relationship". One line was all she needed; he would be her next "date". His approach was so direct, he was too easy. Morana was ready to spend a little more time with Brian.

She walked back to the bed. She had a look in her eyes that told Brian very bad things were about to happen. She had put the soldering iron away, but the hammer was still sitting on the bed. She picked it up and slightly tapped his right knee; she wanted him to know she was back and she was far from finished. He tried to move, but it was useless; he was at her mercy, an emotion she left on Cocoa Beach. She lifted the baton from the table and gave him a short quick jolt to his left knee in order to ensure he was awake. She looked at Brian and, in a calming voice, told him not to worry and that this would all be over soon. She told him he would be free. She knew she would keep her word; she had already made his exit plan.

The blood was out of his eyes now and, through the mirror, he could see her pick up the surgical knife. She grabbed his right leg and wedged a brick under his calf. She took the knife and slid it under his ankle. She slowly sliced through his tendon. She took a rag and wrapped it around his ankle, tying it tightly to contain the bleeding. She slowly walked to the left side of the bed. She asked again if he was starting to realize how it felt to be in pain. She took the brick and put it under his right calf, then slowly sliced through his left tendon. As she wrapped a rag around it, she repeated that it would all be over soon.

There was a pineapple on the kitchen countertop. She walked over and grabbed a kitchen knife and sliced it in half. She sat the two halves down and walked out of the kitchen. She returned with a bottle of liquid Drano. She placed the bottle on the table beside the bed and pulled two hypodermic needles out of her kit. She filled one syringe with Drano. He began to panic. She took his right hand and warned if he moved she would fill the syringe with Drano and shove the needle into each of his testicles. She asked if he understood; he nodded his head up and down. She thanked him for his cooperation.

She took his right hand and, with the rubber tipped pliers, grabbed his index finger at the first knuckle. She stuck the second needle in his fingertip several times. She took his other fingers, sticking them each with the needle and finishing with his thumb. She had purposely aimed for under his nails with decent luck and definitely felt the needle hit bone. For good measure, she stuck his palm several times. She picked the syringe with the Drano up and walked to the left side of the bed, holding both in her hand. She told him he was doing great, but she needed to give him a little reminder what would happen if he moved. She took the needle with the Drano in the syringe and slowly slid it from his nose to his stomach. She stuck it in his belly button and released a small amount. She looked at him and asked if he understood. With a playful smile she said it probably wouldn't be a good idea for him to shake his head no. Staring at him she took the needle out of his stomach and almost laughed as she said he could just blink once for 'yes' or twice for 'no'. After a few seconds, she said she felt comfortable he understood and grabbed his left hand. She took the needle and stuck each finger followed by his palm. She didn't know how many times the needle struck bone but knew it was a lot.

She began to think about Jon and could feel her rage mounting. She stood at the bottom of the bed, grabbed the hammer, and began tapping both of his knees. He couldn't take the pain and turned his head to the right. He could feel the sharp metal pierce his right eye. He centered his head and felt the pain run through his entire body as the metal point ripped through his eye. Within seconds, he realized that any sight left in his right eye after the soldering iron was now permanently gone. Almost unconscious, he tried to jerk himself free from the straps. It was useless, he was absolutely immobile.

11 - GOODBYE BRIAN

She looked at the clock and realized it was almost three o'clock in the morning. She looked at Brian and told him their relationship was coming to an end. She asked him if he was ready to be set free. He tried to nod his head up and down. As she placed her hands on his forehead she told him not to worry. She told him he would no longer have to see the pain he caused people. She grabbed him by his forehead and slowly began turning his head to the left. He tried to fight her but it was futile. He could feel the metal tip slowly go into his left eye. The pain was unbearable, he passed out. She poured chloroform on a rag and placed it over his nose; she wanted to be sure he stayed unconscious.

She rolled the wheelchair she had hidden in the bedroom to the left side of the bed and locked the wheels in place. She undid his straps then lifted Brian's legs over the left side of the bed and placed one hand on the side of each leg. She took plastic tie straps and ran it up each leg tightly securing his wrists, palms out, to each leg. She pulled his body towards her and grabbed under each arm. It took a little effort, but she was able to lift him and place him in the chair. She cleaned the remaining blood off his eyes and put petroleum jelly over them to prevent more bleeding. She took a blanket and placed it over him, tucking the sides under his body covering the fact that he was naked. She slipped his socks and shoes on his feet and placed a big oversized toboggan on his head covering his ears. On top of that she put a baseball cap and pulled the bill down on his face, covering the tinted eye glasses she had placed over his eyes.

She had parked her rental car on the back side of the building out of sight from the road traffic or people. She wheeled him to the elevator and pushed the button to bring it up to her floor. As the door opened, she was relieved to see the elevator was empty. She rolled him and pushed the button for the first floor. She was beginning to feel relief that she felt no guilt, relief that it had been successful; then, the elevator stopped at the 4th floor. As the door opened, she felt a sense of panic. An obviously intoxicated man stumbled in and leaned against the first thing he could find, her wheelchair. Before the man was completely inside, she hit the down button. In a miserable attempt to hit on her, he asked how she was doing on this fine night. She said she was fine and made it a point to avoid eye contact. She could smell alcohol on his breath as he asked what was wrong with her friend. When she didn't reply he reached out and grabbed the bill of the baseball hat. He said he lost a hat just like it tonight and began lifting the hat in an attempt to take it off Brian's head. She put her hand on the top of the hat and forced the bill back over Brian's face. To take his attention away from the guy in the wheelchair, she asked if he had gotten lucky tonight. The elevator couldn't reach the ground floor soon enough. As he began to explain how some bitch had let him buy her drinks all night then wouldn't come home with him, the door opened and she quickly pushed the wheelchair out, leaving the man slumped over still telling his sob story.

As she neared the side door, she noticed two policemen standing on the corner opposite her building. For a brief second, she felt panic but she surprised herself at how quickly it subsided, how quickly she had regained her composure. Going backwards, she pushed the door open and wheeled Brian out. She had to turn the chair and knew he would be facing them but was relieved when they didn't pause in their conversation. She gave a passing glance to the officers, and they seemed uninterested in her or the person she had in the wheelchair. She smiled to herself, wondering if she had been caught could she have bribed them with donuts. She had purposely parked with the passenger side of the car facing the building. Now, she hoped, it would act as a barrier between her and the cops but it wasn't necessary. By the time she reached the passenger door and opened it, the officers had turned the corner and were out of sight. With the wheelchair facing the opened door, she locked the wheels in place and lifted Brian into the car. She was happy she had seen the police; it gave her a little shot of adrenaline, which helped her lift Brian's weight. With Brian in the car, she secured his seat belt, shut the door, and walked to the driver's side ready to head to a special spot she had picked.

Morana and Brian were headed to the mountains of West Virginia. She had every intention of keeping her word; she was going to set Brian free. She used a prepaid Visa gift card to rent a fuel efficient car and filled the tank before parking it at her building. She calculated drive time to West Virginia was close to 9 hours and knew she would only have to stop once for gas. She was going to obey all speed limits. It was 4 AM when she left and soon she was on I-81S in no time. She knew she would enter West Virginia around 2:00 in the afternoon, but didn't want to get to the mountains until 6:00 to ensure it was dark.

She drove around the mountains, periodically stopping to appreciate the fact that the average elevation was 1500 feet above sea level with numerous places that simply dropped off into the Ohio River.

Once she was satisfied it was dark enough, she parked at a very secluded place overlooking the river and retrieved the wheelchair from the trunk. Adrenaline flowing from the excitement someone feels at the conclusion of a first date, she lifted Brian from the car and into the chair. She had applied chloroform several times throughout the trip but, out of pure luck, he began to regain consciousness. She decided once he was out of the car, she would use the rubber tipped pliers and surgical knife to cut out his tongue. She hadn't thought of it until then, but perhaps that could become her trademark. She thought, what better way to prevent these men from making insincere romantic promises they had no intention of keeping?

Thinking about the man in the elevator and seeing the police, she decided Brian would be the only man to leave her apartment alive and visible. Before she changed clothes and began the drive back to New York, she and Brian had to conclude their date. She pushed the wheelchair to the edge of a cliff, locked the wheels, and wrapped duct tape around Brian's elbows, knees, and feet. She hoped he was conscious enough to feel the pain as she ran the tape across each knee cap. She clipped the plastic tie around his right wrist and leg then his left. She could see in his eyes that he was regaining clarity. She leaned down and whispered, "Good bye", as she pushed him out of the chair. As she loaded the wheelchair in the car's trunk, she thought to herself how satisfying it had been to watch him tumble down the side of the cliff before splashing into the freezing water. Goodbye, Brian.

12 - REMORSE

After dropping the wheelchair and her dirty clothes at her Queens apartment, she drove to the rental car place and returned the car. She hailed a cab, went to Grand Central, and then took the subway to 40th street. She didn't think anyone had seen her leave in a car, but didn't want to take any chances; she knew she wouldn't stand out on the subway. She was confident she would go unnoticed returning a day later on foot wearing different clothes. As she was walking into her building, she laughed to herself. She was being a little too paranoid; after all, this was New York City. How many inconspicuous faces did she see everyday?

It was early Sunday and she had been up since Friday morning; she needed to sleep . She wondered if she would be able to. On the drive back from West Virginia, she wondered if she would be able to function as Beth. She reassured herself that Morana wouldn't interrupt her normal life. After all, Beth hadn't killed anyone. She didn't know if her actions would weigh on her conscience or if she would be full of remorse. Neither happened. She had only been in bed a few minutes and could barely keep her eyes open. As she was drifting off to sleep, two thoughts crossed her mind.

She knew Beth was no longer in charge and Brian would be the last to be alive at the end of their "date".

The first thing she did when she awoke was log-on to her online dating account. She checked her inbox and saw the inspiration for the man who would become her next "Date". HungDavid had left her a new message.

13 - HUNGDAVID

It was Sunday evening and as Morana sat in her pajamas sipping wine, her memory shifted from Brian to Jon. Always Jon. She thought about how every new email reminded her of how she had been treated. She recalled how angry she had become with each new message. She recalled how enraged she became with each man who had an ulterior motive. She recalled HungDavid.

She had gotten his first message while Brian was strapped to the bed in her kitchen. She remembered how angry she had become thinking about how hurt his family would be had they known about each of his "friends with benefits" relationships. She was ready to respond.

She reread his one line message. Her response was simple and to the point. She told him she would love to meet, that she was also looking for a relationship with benefits. They were, however, looking for two very different types of benefits.

Morana went out to grab lunch at a little deli near her building. They made the absolute best turkey and avocado sandwich. She ate there frequently. She ordered it the same way each time, on whole wheat with tomatoes lightly toasted. She rarely ate sweets, or any unhealthy food for that matter, but today was different; today was special. She ordered a slice of cheesecake and felt guilty. She almost laughed out loud thinking that, considering her recent actions, it was cheesecake that made her feel guilty. The slice was so good she knew it would be hard to resist next time. She didn't know which made it better, the mascarpone they must have used or the satisfied feeling of knowing one "Jon" would never hurt anyone again. They were all Jon in her mind. She decided it was a little of both.

By the time she got back to her apartment, she had a reply from HungDavid. He was online. She wondered what he was doing on a Sunday evening that allowed him access to a dating profile. Did he not spend time with his wife or kids? Did he have kids? Were they there and he was trying to meet other women right under their noses. She thought the worst of every question she asked herself. Thoughts like these let her do what she did to Brian without feeling remorse for their families. She felt if the families knew what their fathers and husbands were doing, they would thank her. She was doing for them what they wanted to, but couldn't, do for themselves. She felt that way since the second she saw Jon's wife. She felt that way with each "Date".

She opened HungDavid's message and it read "where are you? Let's meet." Always right to the point, she thought. If that was the way he wanted it, she was happy to oblige. Her reply simply said, "I'm in New York. Where are you? Can we meet?" He replied in an instant saying he was in Jersey and could meet ASAP. She thought about ending the conversation; after all Jersey was her backyard. She didn't know if there would be too many obstacles with him being so close. Would there be people who knew he was coming to the city? What if he told them when he was coming/ What if he lied about her address, but not the general area? She knew if they were dumb enough to cheat, they were probably dumb enough to get caught. It wasn't worth the risk if anything could be traced back to her. She thought for a minute realizing she was virtually untraceable. She never used her real anything, always used pre-paid everything, and every piece of technology she had was ultra secure. She knew she would take every measure to avoid making mistakes. Morana never made mistakes. She told herself she would be careful. After all, this time HungDavid wouldn't be set "free" alive. She remembered the old saying--"dead men don't talk". She replied ASAP worked.

13 - JUST LUNCH

She had a busy work week ahead. She didn't want David knowing anything about Beth's life, so she pushed back the chance of any meetings until the following weekend . It was nearing the end of December, just a week before Christmas. She wondered how David would be spending Christmas. She couldn't help thinking about how she would spend Christmas. Her parents were deceased and she had no siblings. Other than a few friends at the office and the occasional visit with old college friends, she spent most of her time alone. She didn't mind being alone and was growing more fond of the solitude. She had a hobby now, a hobby that required a great deal of privacy. She had all but stopped spending time with work friends when she started dating Jon. It always came back to Jon.

How could he have spent so much time with her? How did his family not know? Perhaps he told them he was working. That would explain the trips, but all the phone calls, the emails, the text messages? How was he able to stay in such frequent contact with her and his family not know? How?

She told David they could meet next weekend if he was available. She knew he would be; they always were. He told her that, after seeing her profile picture, he couldn't wait to meet her. He even sounded perverted on email. She couldn't wait to meet him. She asked if he ever came to the city and was relieved when he said almost never. She suggested a restaurant near Time Square. She thought if she was going to be seen with him why not be seen at a place where thousands of other people were being seen. She knew she could be mundane and ensure she didn't stand out. She was confident he wouldn't care if she was made up from head to toe or looked like she had just rolled out of bed; he was there for one reason. So was Morana.

He said the place sounded great and asked her how to get there, a question that made her feel even more comfortable. The fact that he didn't know his way around the city was reassuring. If needed, she planned to take him to different places each time they met. She knew they would run out of "dates" long before they ran out of places to meet. She thought he wouldn't be able to tell anyone where he was going if he didn't know where he was going. She emailed asking for a number, but of course he said he could only contact her via email. She felt he would assume she was married even though her profile said single. If he couldn't give her a number, she suggested, perhaps they shouldn't meet? That was all it took, after even a hint of no willingness on her part to meet, he was all too eager to give her all the numbers she wanted. In his reply, he said it was his work number and his wife would never know. His wife would never know but Morana would.

She called him from her new cell phone and blocked her number. They set a time. The were going to meet for lunch Saturday at one of the delis right in the middle of Time Square. She didn't know if he hadn't protested meeting at the touristy deli because he truly didn't know anything about the city or because he would have said yes to Mars if he thought it would get him laid. She told him she would be wearing jeans, a heavy green coat, and a yellow baseball cap. She said it would be easier for him to spot her in a baseball cap. She simply wanted it to cover her face. He said he had black hair and would be wearing a black leather jacket. Then, in a very braggadocios way, he said he had worn a matching gold necklace and bracelet. She envisioned a 1990's Guido throwback. New Jersey, she could see him now and couldn't help laughing. His profile picture, if it was real, was an up close of only his face. She couldn't resist. She asked him if he wore product and he said yes. He said his hair would be a little spiked on top. Of course it would. She told him to wear a yellow baseball cap so she could spot him. Without hesitation, he said yes. She couldn't wait to see how silly he looked. The only thing bigger than his libido was his ego. She could barely refrain from asking if he was worried it would clash with his gold jewelry.

14 - SECOND FIRST DATE

She hadn't realized how boring Beth's life actually was. She used to get excited when a merger she had put in place finalized or when she signed a new client. Before, it seemed she had just gotten to her office and the work day was ending. Now, she found herself watching the clock and waiting for the markets to close. She hoped for any exciting news that would get the office stirred up. Any event, good or bad, just something to speed up her day. Anything to speed up time, anything to get to her "date" with David. She found that her fast paced job didn't seem so fast paced anymore. A wild swing in the DOW didn't seem to elevate her heart rate. She didn't get anxious when a deal she had worked on seemed as if it was going to fall through.

She found conversations with her coworkers becoming increasingly boring and unimaginative, with the exception of one man. In the past, she had frequently found herself trapped in one sided conversations with this man who had been unquestionably the most boring person in her office, if not all of New York. On far too many occasions, she and several co-workers found themselves trapped, having to listen to one of his many never ending conversations. At the time, Beth didn't realize how entertaining his seemingly pointless conversation around a pineapple would become to Morana. She used to find his mundane rants almost unbearable but not now. He was no longer the most boring person in New York.

Nothing about Beth's job seemed to stimulate her. Nothing about Beth's life was exciting.

It was finally Friday. She realized Friday was the one thing that excited her about Beth's job. She had spent her evenings, and the better part of her days, planning David. The week was finally over and she walked through the door of Morana's apartment. Morana was back; she had never really left.

She sat in front of the one thing that evoked excitement in her life. She logged in and found several new messages from the typical lonely, horny or perverted man. There were two new messages from "HungDavid" in her inbox. She hadn't talked to him since last Sunday and she wondered what his week had been like. He was probably bursting with excitement. She wondered if he had told his friends he was going into the city this weekend. Told them he was about to add another one to the list of women with whom he had cheated on his wife. She knew he would brag about his online dating successes, and she knew she had to take every precaution. She was concerned he would show his friends her profile or tell them where they were meeting.

She wondered if his friends would try to meet her online. She wondered if they would try to indiscriminately come to the city with him to get a glimpse of newest girl notch on his belt. She was going to take steps to ensure the latter didn't happen.

She opened the first of his two messages. The first simply read "can't wait to see you". It seemed so benign that she was emotionless when she read it. David's transparency became crystal clear when she read the second message. Emotion was back, ands she was angry.

In the message, David told her he had been thinking about her all week. He couldn't wait to eat and get back to her place. He said they had all day. Said he told his wife he was going into the city to watch a Nets basketball game with a new guy from work. He told her his wife would never ask questions because the only thing she hated hearing about more than his job was sports.

He said no one knew and that he wanted the relationship to be their little secret. He followed that by asking, in the form of a statement, if she wanted the relationship to be their secret, too, didn't she? In the last line, before the postscript, he had typed "I can trust you, can't I?" Did he really just ask her to trust him? That question alone provided all the incentive she needed.

She read the postscript and settled into a calm rage. It was an intense anger she had never experienced. If she had ever had any doubt about her intentions, they were instantly stifled with just a few words. The postscript read " p.s. …don't wear panties. My wife doesn't, and I love that shit." When she read the postscript, she knew she had to change her original agenda. This guy was worth the extra thought she was now going to put into their "date".

It was late Friday evening, and if she

were going to modify her plans for David, she needed to get started. They were meeting the next day at 6:00; she had 18 hours.

15 - THE YELLOW HAT

A little before 5:00 on Saturday, she called David and told him she needed to meet at another restaurant. She had to run an errand, and it would be much more convenient for her. He should have been on his way to the city by now and the last minute change should make it harder for any of his friends should they be following him. She hoped it would also throw off his sense of direction. It was a little trickier to find a restaurant on 60th street than Time Square. She wanted a restaurant on 60th street in order to be close to the F train. She wanted to meet and get back to Morana's place in Queens quickly, and she knew David wouldn't mind. Even though it was New York, the fewer people that saw them together the better. She told him anytime of the day she loved omelets from the restaurant called Serendipity 3 and wanted him to meet her there. She said pretty please and acted schoolgirl excited. She was confident if she acted like he was doing her a favor he wouldn't hesitate and would expect a favor in return. Of course he said yes. Men, she thought to herself. What a strange and predictable gender.

They planned to meet at 6:00, but she got there around 5:45. She didn't go into the restaurant until 5:57. She looked around, although she didn't really know why. She didn't plan on doing anything out of the ordinary. In fact, she wanted quite the opposite. She wanted to go completely unnoticed. She waited to go into the restaurant until she could see a man with a black leather jacket and yellow baseball cap approaching. She was waiting on him when he stepped into the place. She hadn't worn a yellow hat. She didn't want him to notice her until she had noticed him. She thought for a second, and kind of regretted asking him to wear one. Her idea had worked a little too well; he stood out a little.

She stepped up to him and asked if he was David. He replied and said no he was HungDavid. She was so ready, it was all she could do to smile and introduce herself. She asked if he had any trouble finding the place and was he hungry? In a very typical, trying to be macho way, he said he never had problems with directions and that he didn't care if they ate or just went back to her place. She ordered an omelet to go; they really were delicious. It was Saturday and there were plenty of people out. The first thing she did after she ordered her omelet was take off his hat, telling him she wanted to see his hair. He went off on some spiel about how he used two kinds of product. They couldn't get to her apartment fast enough.

16 - THE VERSATILE BAGMAN

Morana found that drug dealers were a better resource than the internet for many items that weren't "readily available". Dealers had no paper trail. They certainly weren't going to report you to the authorities, and could typically get a product more quickly than the internet. They were generally more expensive, but tended to be very reliable as long as you had the money. She met a very resourceful (and what turned out to be very useful) dealer soon after renting Morana's apartment. Beth had never actually met a drug dealer and their first meeting was innocent enough; she didn't realize how their relationship would grow. She knew the coffee shop tech guy wouldn't be able to get the things she needed, outside of technology. Now, thanks to her many visits to the library, she was learning about lots of new things. The first time they met, she heard him offering snow cones to people as they walked by. Her white collar co-workers didn't exactly keep her apprised of the latest street jargon. She didn't know what "snow cone" meant, but there wasn't a snow cone machine in sight. Given the fact he was outside in freezing weather, and wearing clothes four times too big for him, she felt comfortable he wasn't the head of a Queen's snow cone conglomerate.

He was an overweight Latino dressed in black baggy jeans. He had on several shirts, covered by an oversized University of Chapel Hill sweatshirt. Pulled down covering half his face he was wearing a Duke baseball cap, which perplexed her just a bit. He also had, what she assumed were gang related, tattoos. She didn't know how many were covered by his clothing, but she could see several on his hands and neck. She didn't notice until she had already walked over to him, and didn't know if they had any specific meaning, but he appeared to have two small teardrops under his eye. She knew from a documentary she had seen on gang violence he was probably someone to be feared. Had she noticed the tear drops, she would have never approached him. But it was too late, she was committed. She had entered his personal space and it was obvious she was about to speak.

She had no intention of buying drugs. She sincerely wanted to know why he was offering passers-by snow cones. Between her job and personality, she was a very confident woman. She had sat in front of CEOs, multi-millionaires, and some of the most powerful men in New York, none of which intimidated her. She thought the best way to find out what he was actually selling was to ask for a snow cone. As soon as she asked the questions, she realized she was saying it with a timid voice. She didn't realize she was actually a little intimidated until she spoke.

She wasn't sure what to expect. She thought maybe he would pull a gun out and say she was 5.0, or tell her to get lost and threaten her. She thought of all the movie scenes and how wrong it went for the stranger who asked for anything from a drug dealer. Was he even a drug dealer? Maybe he had a live one and was going to explain how his wife had just died or his car had broken down, or any of the other thousand excuses she had heard, but all would be just fine if she would lend him a dollar. She was watching this man standing on the street, looking her up and down, and her only thought now was why would they even say that. The pan handler knows the are never going to pay the dollar back.

He opened his mouth to answer her, and she was surprised. He actually spoke a language she understood, English, and used proper grammar. He didn't speak some coded gangster language using the f word every other syllable. He didn't speak

Mexican to try to get her to leave him alone. He didn't even speak in a mean or threatening tone.

He looked at her shoes and purse and replied "lady you don't want a snow cone". She realized she had made a mistake, she was wearing Beth's cloths. Needing to take the focus away from her appearance as quickly as possible, she said he was right, she wanted two. He said she didn't look like a beamer, and she surely didn't look like a bag bride. Now she was really confused. She didn't know what snow cone, beamer, or bag bride meant.

She was pretty sure his definition of a beamer was a little different than hers. Trying to be persuasive, she told him she was. He just laughed and asked her what she really wanted. She thought for a second. She realized this was his office and her great ability to bluff wouldn't work here. Knowing she probably didn't look like any of those things, and feeling less threatened after hearing him speak, she just asked him what a snow cone was. Surmising she wasn't the police, he told her if she were a cop she deserved an Oscar. It took her a second to understand what he meant, but couldn't help **smiling** when she got the joke. He knew she was harmless and couldn't resist the temptation to mess with her a little. He said a snow cone was candy. You know, bubble gum. She was clueless. Trying not to look as clueless as she was she asked who would want a snow cone. He said puffers. Now she was actually getting mad, not at him but at the fact that she had no idea what he was talking about. In Beth's world, she was expected to know everything, and generally did.

Feeling evermore at ease, she said just tell me what a snow cone is in English. He looked at her and said a snow cone is crack. She had seen and heard plenty of people trying to sell crack, but had never hear it called a snow cone. She asked him what the other terms meant. He told her candy was another name for crack and a bag bride was a crack prostitute. Knowing he had been messing with her she said maybe I am a bag bride, you don't know. He laughed and said he had 10 dollars. She asked what a beamer or a puffer fish were. He said a beamer was a crack user and a puffer fish was a Tetraodontidae. She thought he was messing with her again and making up words to see if she would fall for it. She told him to forget it, if he wasn't going to tell her she didn't care. She just wanted to know what a snow cone was. He kind of laughed and said I told you. A puffer is a crack user but you asked me what a puffer fish was and a puffer fish is a member of the Tetraodontidae Family. She asked if that were true and if so how he knew that. He told her it was true and he knew because he paid attention in school.

He probably noticed the slight look of

bewilderment on her face. She asked what school he had gone to. He said he was still in school taking classes at Queens College. This guy had surprised her again. The bewilderment had to be obvious at this point. He got a little defensive and said that's right, I go to college. I guess because I sell drugs you think I can't be smart. She was a little stumped. She found herself rooting for a drug dealer and you're not supposed to root for a drug dealer. She said "I think it's great you go to school, but why do you sell drugs?" He told her he had no family. He said he hated selling drugs. He never knew his father and his life had been hard. He grew up with his mother, if you wanted to call her that, who'd been a bag bride. He had a little brother he had to take care of financially, not to mention paying for college. He told her he had been admitted to The University of Syracuse, but couldn't afford tuition. He was trying to save enough money to transfer. He wanted his little brother to have a better life.

He looked at her and said "Now that you know my life story, what's the deal with you?" She quickly snapped back to her reality. She felt sorry for this guy having to take care of his brother while trying to go to school, but she couldn't think about that. She had to be unassuming and forgettable Morana, and Morana had no feelings.

She told him she was a receptionist in the city, and that she didn't really go out much or do anything exciting. She said she hadn't gone to college, but always wished she had. He looked at her like he knew she was lying. He asked where she worked. Morana would have never told anyone the name of her actual employer, but Beth was so focused on the new slang she was learning she went blank. Realized she was pausing, and not wanting him to think she was lying, she blurted out the name of her firm. She regretted it before she finished saying the name. Almost instantly, she thought of three offices she could have said but it was too late; he knew something real about her.

Looking at her, he said he didn't know too many receptionists that sport a Louis Vuitton purse and Prada shoes. "Let me guess," he said. "Your parents are rich, but you just love living in Queens so much you didn't want to stay in the city. You're showing them right, you don't need them. You can do everything on your own, as long as they pay for your clothes, purses, furniture, rent and everything else. That's all right he said, I keep it real with you but you can't be straight up with me."

She did feel bad lying to this guy, but she couldn't tell him the truth. She found it easy to like him. She would never take the chance, but couldn't help thinking if she did tell him about her alternate life, he wouldn't judge her and would probably even keep her secret. Of course, she would never take that risk. She leaned in a little and asked him if he could keep a secret. He said I sell drugs and you are asking me if I can keep a secret. She told him she had a little shopping problem and just maybe used her credit cards a little too much. He smiled at her and said sure.

She said she had to go but would talk to him later. She turned to walk away and realized they hadn't actually introduced themselves. She looked back and said I don't even know your name. He said they call me Chino, and you are. She paused and said they call me Morana then kept walked towards her building. After a few steps she heard him say Morana. She looked back and he said I am smart but I know about the puffer fish because some weird guy asked me to find one for him a while back. She asked if he really sold a guy a puffer fish. He said if you can afford it I can get it.

It was date night. She and David took the subway back to her apartment. She had rolled the fold up bed back into the bedroom, but didn't plan on leaving it there long. She asked if he wanted a drink. In predictable fashion, he said anything with alcohol. He asked where the bathroom was, said he had to piss. She hated this man a little more every time he opened his mouth. She pointed to the bathroom and told him she would make them drinks. When he left the room, she made him a vodka tonic. She took some Dormicum out of her purse and dropped it in his drink.

She had been prescribed 7.5mg tablets of Dormicum when work related stress prevented her from sleeping but only took it once, but she didn't like how groggy and irascible it made her feel the next day. Her initial intent was to use GHB, but could find no drug that would definitely reverse its effect. She read that Naloxone had in tests, but that it failed to in other studies. She didn't want to take any chances. She was new to these drugs and didn't know the difference between enough and too much.

While she was waiting on David, she wondered to herself if Chino would have been able to get the drug for her, or any prescription drug for that matter. She remembered Chino saying "I told you, if you can afford it I can get it". She would come to realize how much she was underestimating what Chino was capable of procuring. She could hear him now asking why she needed Midazolam. He would have called it Midazolam; after all, he paid attention in school.

She asked the doctor who prescribed the Dormicum if there was anything she could use to counter its effect. She explained she couldn't afford the drowsiness it caused. He prescribed her Flumazenil, but mentioned it was available in injection form only. She filled the prescriptions but never used the drug.

She made herself a vodka and cranberry in a small glass. She made David's drink very strong. She knew he would never admit it was too strong; after all, he was a tough guy. She put just enough vodka in hers to give it the taste of alcohol. She mixed it with water to dilute it while making it look bigger than it actually was. David walked out of the bathroom and asked if she wanted to make this a regular thing. He said he could probably get away from his wife and come into the city twice a week. She thought to herself how glad she was she didn't have a gun, a bullet wasn't good enough for this guy. It took all the effort she had, but managed a fake smile and said let's see how today goes. She knew if it went well there would be no more trips to the city for David.

She told him to have a seat and enjoy his drink, she was going to freshen up. She gave David his drink and went in the bathroom with hers. The drug couldn't work fast enough. She could hear the ice moving and knew he was drinking. He shouted to her that it was a good drink and that the alcohol would make it better for her. He said getting a little drunk really helped his stamina, not that he needed it of course. She hoped he would have plenty of stamina. She didn't want him to miss out on one moment of the time she planned on spending with him.

She walked back into the den after a few minutes. She tried her best to make pleasant conversation until the drink kicked in. She didn't know how long it would take the Drug to work. She had put three times what the doctor prescribed for her in his drink. She read that it worked in as fast as 15 minutes. She didn't want him to realize he had been drugged and have enough time to leave her apartment. She was afraid she would have to pretend to be sexually interested in him in order to make him stay if he tried to leave.

She could tell he was beginning to get groggy. He asked what was in his drink and she said nothing, it was just a very strong drink. She started talking about his stamina and how he had said it was improved with alcohol. He started to look confused, but she didn't want him to question the effects of the drug. She unbuttoned her blouse and asked what he wanted to do to her and if she was going to like what he wanted her to do to him. She thought he would be less likely to be concerned about his reaction to the drug if she was able to get him to focus on sex. It appeared to be working. He leaned over to feel her breast but couldn't quite raise his arm. He said he wanted to tie her up. She couldn't help smiling at the irony of him wanting to tie her up.

It had only been 10 minutes, he had finished his drink too quickly. He stood up and again asked what she had put in his vodka. He was wobbly, but coherent enough to realize something was wrong. She took her top off hoping he would focus on her, but he started walking towards the door. Unlike Brian, he was stronger than her, but she couldn't let him make it out of the apartment. She stood up and grabbed his arm, but he pushed her back onto the couch. He was steps away from the door. She realized just how small the place really was. She wrapped her arms around him from the back, but it was too late, he had already turned the doorknob. The door opened inward, causing him to take a step back. She could almost pull him back into her hallway. He stepped out into the corridor and stumbled into the door of the apartment adjacent hers. She could tell the drug was working, just another minute or two. If she could just get him back into the apartment. She could hear the door opening.

She had only seen her neighbor once. She was a small elderly woman who lived alone. She only noticed she lived across from her because she saw her new drug dealer friend Chino carrying her groceries into her apartment. Who knew, a college student drug dealer who helped the elderly with their groceries. She hadn't met Chino at the time but remembered it was him after they talked earlier that day. In Beth's world, a guy like Chino stood out. A thousand suits could walk by her and she wouldn't be able to recall one, but a guy in black baggy pants with four shirts? That she remembered.

Her neighbor cracked the door just a little and asked if everything was ok. She asked if she needed to call the police. She quickly replied "no" and explained he was just her friend who had a little too much to drink. The woman noticed she wasn't wearing a shirt and stared at them both before accepting her explanation and shutting the door. David mumbled the word "help". Had her neighbor shut her door completely? Had she heard him? Was she going to call the police?

Finally, the drug worked; David was losing consciousness. He fell towards her apartment door and she was able to pull him into her hall. She shut the door behind her, wondering if her neighbor was watching through her peephole. She tried to reassure herself. This was New York, people constantly walk: by drug dealers, muggers, and crack addicts without batting an eyelash. Surely an old lady wouldn't want to get involved with a lover's quarrel.

She wasn't sure how long the drug would keep him asleep. She knew from this point on she would use stronger drugs that worked much faster. She thought maybe should stick with the stun gun and chloroform. She wanted to get to work, she could feel the adrenaline. She began to undress him, but left his gold chain on; she thought it may come in handy for some of the tools she planned on using to help cure David of his adulterous ways.

She rolled the bed beside the couch. She had managed to pull him on top and locked the wheels. She put her chest on his and her arms under his arms. He was heavier than Brian, but she had enough adrenaline flowing through her to lift five men.

The fact that they were face to face when she pushed him on the bed almost made her nauseous. What if, while waiting on the drug, she'd had no choice but to kiss him? She grabbed him under his knees, lifting his legs onto the bed. Even though he was harder to move than Brian, she was able to pull him up and position him on the bed. She crossed his legs and wrapped the strap around his left ankle, then around and back under his right ankle. She tightened the strap and secured both sides to the bed frame. For good measure, she took a pair of handcuffs she had purchased at a nearby gun store and secured his ankles together. The things they will let anyone buy she thought. She pulled his arms out until he was in a t-shape and strapped his left wrist to the bed frame. She looped the straps around his chest, underneath the bed, and back over his chest before securing his right wrist to the bed. She took a final strap and ran it across his forehead, securing it as tightly as possible to prevent his head from moving. She double checked each strap until she was confident he wasn't able to move. To prevent him from talking, she took duct tape and wrapped it tightly several times around his head and mouth, noticing what was becoming a bald spot. She laughed, almost wishing he were awake so they could discuss his dwindling need for product. Reassured he was immobile and couldn't scream, she walked into the bedroom to get her "date" kit.

She saw his breathing began to slow and took the syringe of Flumazenil out of her bag. She had guessed at his body weight and hoped she hadn't put too much of the Midazolam in his drink. She had researched the amount needed based on a person's body size but knew the drug could cause respiratory problems if the correct amount wasn't administered. She had given him a lot, maybe too much. She checked to be sure the duct tape was tight over his mouth and gave him the injection. She wasn't sure how much of the drug it would take to reverse the Dormicum, so she started with a small amount. She read that it should begin working in as quickly as 1-2 minutes and knew she could administer additional injections if needed. She waited five minutes, it didn't seem to be working. She gave him a second shot with double the dose of the first, within two minutes he began to awake. She realized how well the combination worked. It would be easier next time.

18 - HUNG DAVID'S DATE

She was standing over him as he regained consciousness. He realized he was immobile. He tried to scream, but his sounds were muffled. He quickly realized no one would hear him. Another "Date" was at her mercy. She thought how ideal it would be to take a picture of him with the panic radiating from his eyes and use it as his new online profile. The same profile he used to meet women so he could have adulterous affairs. The profile he used that, if they knew, would devastate the lives of those closest to him, those who were supposed to be the most important in his life. The thought faded, she knew he would never use his profile again

She wondered how this macho man felt now. He made futile attempts to move, he was helpless. She looked at him and asked how it felt to have no control. She asked if he thought his wife liked the feeling of having no control over his adulterous life. She told him if he had been faithful he could be with his family right now. If he had been faithful he wouldn't be naked, strapped to a bed in the kitchen of an untraceable woman. She wanted him to be aware of the fact she had created the woman he thought would be the next notch on his belt. She had created the woman who couldn't be found. She thanked him for following all of her last minute instructions to ensure no one knew what he was doing and where he was doing it. She told him it had worked, if there was any one who actually cared enough about him to look they would never find him, they wouldn't even know where to start. She told him he had no idea how much he was about to wish he had been faithful.

She took the stun baton and put the end on his gaudy gold chain. She gave him a quick shock, and could see he felt the electricity running through his body. She knew there was a good chance he would vomit before she was done with him. She didn't want him to choke on his own regurgitation. Dying that way would be too good for him and too quick for her. She told him he had been the one inflicting pain, but that was about to change. Looking through the mirror on the ceiling, he could see her date kit. He watched as she removed a ball peen hammer and a pair of pliers. He could see a surgical knife and a large serrated knife. He could see several bottles of fluid but couldn't tell what they were. When he saw her take an ice pick out of the kit, he tried to move his arms and legs. He tried to jerk, to pull any part of his body free but it was useless, she had secured him too tightly. She stood beside the table, blocking any view he had of the kit. She said she had a few special things for him and asked if he liked surprises.

Using a towel, she covered the items on the table and walked over to the kitchen counter. The counter was out of the view of the mirror, but could hear water running and the clink of glass. She turned and walked back to the side of the bed holding a small bowl. She sat it down on the table and asked if he was ready. He was horrified but could do nothing. She took the ice pick and placed the tip on his left testicles. She pressed a little. She told him not to worry and removed the ice pick. She could see the relief in his eyes until she placed the tip on his thigh. She pushed the ice pick down through the skin of his leg until it was touching bone. She moved her hand in a small circular motion with the tip scraping his femur bone. She pulled the ice pick out and could tell he was crying. She reminded him of the stamina he had promised her. She assured him he would need it.

She put the ice pick down, for now, and sat in a chair she had pushed aside to make room for the bed. Her pensive look terrified him. Tilting his head forward, he could see the look of anger in her expression. She walked over to her laptop, which was sitting on the counter. She logged into her profile and opened HungDavid's message. She looked at him and read his message out loud. Married, looking for a "friends with benefits" relationship. Staring into his eyes, she walked back to the bedside whispering it was the married that got her attention but the benefits were why he was here.

She wedged his legs apart and tried to place a small narrow pipe between the inside of his thighs. With what little room he had he wiggled his legs preventing the pipe from staying in place. She picked the ice pick up and asked if he needed help keeping his legs still. He shook his head no and she tried to place the pipe between his thighs again. He moved his legs again, preventing the pipe from staying in place.

She told him he could have it his way. She took a small blow torch she had concealed under the bed and lit it. With the pipe, she lifted his chain from his neck and began to heat it with the flame. He was terrified. She asked if it was real gold or fake like every other thing in his life. As the chain was heating, she asked what temperature he thought would melt gold. She reassured him, she wasn't going to melt his gaudy gold necklace. She purposely used the word necklace. She lifted the corner tip of the sheet he was lying on and held it to the chain long enough for him to see it was about to ignite. She removed the sheet, then removed the pipe. The chain was just long enough to come to rest on his upper chest. He could smell the hairs burning. His eyes were begging her to stop. She asked if he thought he would be able to keep his legs still and he shook his head yes. She placed the pipe between his thighs, this time he laid perfectly still. She took a belt and wrapped it around both legs, pulling it as tight as the pipe would let her. His legs were spread as far as the restraints allowed and the pipe ensured they didn't close. She took the prod and gave the pipe a shock. She let the pain run through his body. Sarcastically, she told him he looked like a good guy so if he moved she would let him choose between the prod or the pick to help him remember to stay still.

She stood up to get a piece of sandpaper she had under her kitchen sink when she heard a knock at the door. She froze for a minute and thought back to her neighbor. Had the little old lady come to check on her? She walked down the hall towards the door. She looked back to be sure the bed is far enough in the kitchen to not be visible. She has her hand on the doorknob when she glances out her peephole. She expected to see her neighbor but almost froze when she realized it was the police. She recognized one of the officers. He had been standing on the corner the night she took Brian to her car. She looked different, she wasn't wearing the same wig. She hoped he wouldn't recognize her. She hadn't turned the doorknob and hoped they would leave if she didn't answer. She moved her head away from the peephole standing perfectly still, not making a sound. After what seemed like hours, she began to regain her composure when she heard her neighbor tell the police she knew someone was in the apartment. She had no choice, she had to open the door.

She greeted the officers and asked what she could do for them. They were peering down her hallway as they explained the woman in the corridor with them called saying it looked as if a man was attacking you. In her best attempt to show there were no problems she moved aside so the officers had an unimpeded view of the hall. She explained her boyfriend had been there earlier, but was drunk and got a little angry when she made him leave. She said they caught her right as she was about to turn the lights out and head to bed. She instantly thought of three different words she could have used other than caught.

David could hear everything and was trying, in vain to scream, or rattle the bed. The duct tape wrapped around his head and covering his mouth prevented even the slightest sound. The bed was on rollers but they were locked in place. What little movement he could manage was to no avail.

She began to get nervous as a tenant several doors down stepped out of his apartment. She was attracting attention, the exact thing she constantly tried to avoid. For a brief second, Beth came racing back; bluffing was part of her daily life. Her explanations seemed to satisfy everyone in the corridor. She breathed the smallest sigh of relief as the police turned to walk away. The first officer hadn't finished saying call if she needed anything before the second interrupted him and said he smelled something burning. David's chest hair, how could she explain the smell. She calmly said the first thought that came into her head. She told the officer she had left her curling iron on. She had a busy day and had to get started early so she considered doing her hair tonight to save time but was too tired. She must have forgotten to turn it off. There was a brief pause then the officer closest to her said he was glad he was bald, he didn't have to worry about those pesky curling irons anymore. She gave them a big smile and slowly closed the door as they walked away. She leaned against the wall feeling confident that, like so many times before, she had been able to talk her way out of a problematic situation. That feeling quickly faded and was replaced by anger as she headed back to the kitchen thinking about David and how he had caused yet another problem.

She retrieved the sandpaper and began to furiously rub it on his knee. She rubbed until the skin was scratched open and bleeding. She picked up a squirt bottle filled with liquid. He could see the words Muriatic Acid written in black permanent marker. She slowly poured the fluid over his knee and watched as the pain shot up his body. He felt like every nerve in his body felt the sting. She stopped pouring and promised not to pour acid on any opened wound. She smiled and told him it was only lemon juice. She knew psychologically the thought of acid on his open skin would make it much more painful. She sat the bottle down and poured a little water over his knee. She looked at him and said see some pain is only temporary, some pain. She picked up a second squirt bottle and said, "Unfortunately, some pain lasts forever.

She had purchased a gas mask at a military second hand shop and as she put it on, he could see the bottle had no label.

She took the small bowl and filled it half way. She looked at him, smiling, and said she knew he wanted to use these today. He realized she was looking at his genitals and began shaking his head left and right as much as his restraints allowed.

She placed the bowl on the table and put rubber gloves on. She told him they needed to go over a few simple instructions. She pulled out her needle nose pliers and pointed them towards his penis. She told him she was going to put his balls in a bowl she had created especially for him. Of course there are rules she said and the one I suggest you adhere to the most is rule one, no moving. She asked David if he could do that and saw the fear in his eyes as his head stayed motionless. She grabbed the head of his penis with the pliers and told him the second rule is easier than the first; if you move you will be reminded of rule one in a very memorable way.

She lifted the bowl to his face and pointed out two small holes at the top on opposite sides. She pulled out three twist ties from her pocket and a little black case with a silver snap. She asked if he could guess what was in the case. She told him she wouldn't use what was inside if he could tell her what it was. She paused for a moment then looked into his eyes and asked how he liked not being able to use him mouth. Not being able to use the one thing he thought he used so smoothly. She said, "Having that mouth is worthless the one time it could actually benefit someone. It is a shame, too, since you are the person who would be the benefactor."

She stepped just out of his line of sight, snapped the snap, and opened the case. She slowly pulled out something he could tell was shiny, but could only see with his peripheral vision. She stepped back in front of him and threaded the little holes in the bowl with the twist ties then looked down with raised eyebrows and an excited look on her face, then turned back to the case.

She grabbed the glue off the "date" table and returned to the bowl. His mind raced. She was making virtually no noise and almost no movement. He was petrified of not knowing what she was doing with that bowl, that bowl she said she was going to place his nuts in. She turned around, he saw the special bowl and immediately knew what she meant by rule one. She squirted a little glue in the bowl, lifted his balls, and placed them in it, twisting the bowl slightly. Once she was satisfied his scrotum adhered to the bowl, she took the glue and placed a small amount on the straight razor she had attached to one of the twist ties. She told him making his bowl was inspired when she read his "don't wear panties" email. She said after that email I knew whatever I planned for you would be fun. Now back to your scrotum and it's new little house.

She had one of the ties twisted through the hole where the handle of the razor used to be and was holding the other tie in the glue on the opposite end of the razor. Once she had his scrotum glued to the bowl and the roof of his little penis house positioned on top of his penis, she took the 3rd twist tie and used it to twist the first two tightly together. She told him she didn't want the roof to fall off his new little house if he started to get wiggly.

She grabbed a clear transparent plastic bottle off the table and he could see it was partially full of a clear liquid, but the bottle wasn't labeled. She looked down and told him not to worry, this wasn't lemon juice. She put the gas mask on, opened the bottle, and slowly poured the fluid into the bowl. As she poured, she explained that muriatic acid was relatively safe and painless, as long as you rinse it thoroughly with water as soon as it makes contact with the skin. She said she recently read it took about 10 seconds for the acid to begin to burn the skin. She told him when it started to burn to speak up and she would rinse it thoroughly with water. She looked down at him and smiling said remember, all you have to do is speak up.

HungDavid lay there with his scrotum slowly beginning to burn, realizing the pain was going to get much worse and thinking about what would happen if he tried to shake the special bowl off his body. The thought of not being able to move made the pain that much worse and as his groin began to burn, he couldn't help trying to shake the bowl off and in the mirror could see the razor making small cuts over his penis. He looked **as if** he were going to pass out, she was confident the bowl had done its job.

She undid all the twist ties and removed the "roof" of the house. She used a rag to absorb the acid and placed it in a mason jar, which she then sealed and put on the table. She rinsed the bowl several times with hot water each she could see the pain in his eyes. She looked over to the acid sitting on the table and told him they may need that again if he didn't behave. She looked at him and told him he would have a nasty scar but not to worry, no one would ever see it then walked into the den and opened the window. She placed a fan facing out to clear the fumes and took off the gas mask.

She took some smelling salt and rubbed it under his nose. She told him the fun was only beginning and she didn't want him to miss one minute. Once she was sure he was fully conscious she told him it was time for one for one of those surprise she had told him about. She told him to get comfortable and walked out of the room. He could hear her. He could tell she had gone into the bathroom and panicked at the thought of what might be next. For a few minutes he heard no movement. He laid there feeling the pain of the acid on his thighs and groin. With every second of silence the only thing he felt more than the burn from the acid was the fear of when she would return.

She walked back into the room holding a curling iron. He panicked and was quickly reminded he couldn't move. He couldn't escape. He had no control of a situation he knew was about to worsen. She grabbed his right hand, which he immediately balled into a fist. Looking into his eyes, she said "**n**ot yet." She told him to open his hand. He didn't, **so** she took the iron and laid in on his knee. He tried to move his body, but it seemed as if the straps were getting tighter with every jerk. He could feel the iron burning his knee and opened his hand. She took the iron and placed it on his palm. "Now you can make a fist," she said. The heat was so intense. The thought raced through his head; what would she do if he didn't do as he was told. He couldn't do it, he refused to make a fist. She removed the iron and picked up the plastic tube up. She told him if he didn't want to know what the tube was for he should make a fist. Holding the ice pick, she walked to the opposite side of the bed. She placed the tip on his thigh and told him to close his hand. He remembered the feel of the pick scraping his bone and she noticed a tear for the first time as he closed his hand. She held the tube over his left eye and he straightened his fingers. She took the surgical knife from her kit and made small incisions down each finger tip jabbing the tip into his fist each time he closed his hands. Once all five fingertips had been cut she placed the iron on his palm again **and** told him to make a fist. Slowly, she said. He could feel the burning heat on each finger as the curling iron touched the cuts. After a few seconds, she could smell his skin burning and removed the curling iron. She sat it on the table and left the room again.

He wanted to pass out but his body, and worse his mind, was staying awake. In what seemed like an instant, she came back into the room. She was holding the small blow torch and it was lit. She told him not to worry, he wouldn't feel the burn from the curling iron in a few minutes. She put the flame to the metal pipe between his legs and turned it on high. It took a few seconds, but he could feel the pipe getting hot on both sides. He was able to move his legs slightly but the pipe was so secure it moved with him. It didn't take long until both sides of the pipe were burning into his thighs. She left the flame on the metal, looking at him and said "I told you you'd forget all about the curling iron." As she stared at HungDavid, she realized she was beginning to enjoy this. For a second she thought about Beth, and knew she was no longer that person. She had become Morana and Morana was now in complete control of both lives.

18 -GOODBYE HUNGDAVID

Standing beside the bed, looking at David, the only thought in her mind was how badly he deserved this. He should suffer like the ones he had hurt suffered. She decided he was going to do just that. She knew she wouldn't let another "Date" have a chance at freedom but that didn't change the fact that first they needed to be on the receiving end of pain before she relived them from their suffering. She couldn't cause the emotional pain they did, but she had every intention of causing the physical.

She removed the flame from the pipe. He laid there unable to move. His knees were burning from the pipe, his thighs and groin were burning from the acid but she was far from done.

She tore a piece of duct tape and wrapped it over his eyes. She wanted to torture him psychologically as well as physically. He could hear her moving around in the kitchen but couldn't tell what she was doing. He could feel his heart rate elevate as the fear from not being able to see increased with every noise she made. He could hear her move around the kitchen for what seemed like an eternity. He heard the sound of a refrigerator door open and water running. He became more panicked with each noise. He heard her walk back to the bed. By the time he realized she was standing beside him she already had her hand on the tape. She ripped the tape from his right eye. He grimaced as he felt his eyebrow being ripped from his face. Looking in the mirror he could see little specks of blood where his eyebrow used to be. She put one glove and her mask back on then took the muriatic acid and squirted a small amount on a piece of rag. She placed the rag where his eyebrows once was then put the duct tape back over his eye. She held some more smelling salt under his nose to ensure he stayed with her.

He couldn't see, the tape was still covering his eyes, but he could tell she picked something up from the floor and sat in on the bed. She ripped the tape from his eyes again then walked over to the sink and got a glass of water. She poured the water over his eyes, she wanted to be sure his vision was restored. As his eyes recovered he realized the item she placed on the bed was a bored. She walked back to the chair and sat down. She wanted to give his brain a few minutes to think about what might be next.

She could tell he was trying to scream through the tape that covered his mouth. He was probably trying to beg for mercy she thought. Why should she show him any mercy. He seemed guilt free from the pain he caused for so many. She could only imagine how many there were before her.

With the thought of his actions and the

actions of men like him she decided to let him suffer before concluding their date. She sat in front of her laptop and opened her profile. She hadn't finished with HungDavid but could already feel the excitement as she sat there thinking of the atrocities she had planning for her next date, whomever the deserving man may be. There were over a dozen new emails but she was looking for one in specific. She had earmarked an email from the man she called the lotto guy. She sent a short, to the point, reply. The reply simply read, if you have lottery money you can have me. She was angry again, she was ready to spend more time with David. She got up and walked back to the bed.

She poured water over the pipe and yanked it from his thighs. She picked up two bricks from under the bed. Standing on his right side of the bed she forced one brick horizontally under his left knee. The straps were so tight she could barely force the second brick vertically under his right knee.

She took a bottle of wood glue she had placed on the table and poured it over both knees. She placed the bored over both of his knees and pushed down with her hand holding it in place until the glue dried. He was so scared he almost didn't feel the pain of the board on his sandpapered knees. She pulled the towel off the table exposing the rest of the items in her date kit. Looking through the mirror he could see she had a hammer and several nails. She sat the hammer on the board. With her right hand she took a nail and raked it across his chest where the chain had burned his skin then laid it on his stomach. She could see his eyes widen as she picked the hammer up. He tried to lean his head up to see what she was about to do but the strap was too tight, he could only look into the mirror.

She lifted the hammer and wrapped it with cloth that had covered her date kit. She took the nail and placed it on the board directly above his right knee. She gave the nail a slight tap then paused for a second. She enjoyed watching the panic in his face and realized imposing psychological fear was almost as exhilarating as inflicting physical pain. She walked to the top of the bed and stared into his eyes for a moment before walking back to the table. She picked up the nail and placed it in the middle of the board. She began to hammer. With each swing of the hammer his knees felt as if they were going to shatter. She got the first nail in the board and grabbed a second one. She nailed it. It felt as if both kneecaps had been crushed. She took the belt from his pants and wrapped it around his shins then began to tighten it slowly. The tighter it got the more he could feel the skin from his knees being ripped from the glue holding the board in place. She explained the belt wasn't going to be able to tighten as much as she'd like, the boards would have to be removed.

She leaned over him and grabbed the board

with both hands. She could see the acid was still burning the skin in his groin. She pulled the board off his left knee ripping skin with it. She looked at him and told him the other knee was next. She waited for a few seconds, just long enough for him to anticipate the pain. She ripped the board off his right knee. Once it was completely off she wedged the pipe back between his thighs then tightened the strap bringing his legs closer together with the pipe digging into his skin. She loosened the straps and sat the board back on his legs then picked the hammer up. She hammered until the tip of one nail pierced thru the other side. She placed the bored on his legs with the nail touching his skin and slammed it with the hammer. He could feel the nail rip into his skin. She hit the bored a second time and could fill the nail hit bone. She ran smelling salt below his nose and told him she had to run an errand but would be back soon. She told him she had another one of those previously mentioned surprises.

She looked down at him with the board hammered into his left leg thinking about how the skin above his eye was slowly dissolved by acid. She realized the more pain she inflicted the more she wanted to inflict. She thought by causing them to suffer the anger would subside but it didn't, quite the opposite. She had changed. She smiled and walked out of the kitchen.

19 - THE CHEST

She knew she would need a large chest. She had gone to a local hardware store but couldn't find any that were both large and sturdy enough to meet her needs. She didn't want to buy anything online to avoid any trail back to her computer, she used cash and a credit card would provide too much personal information. She found a website where she could buy a large cedar trunk on wheels, and pay by phone.

With David strapped to a bed in her kitchen, she went to her usual convenience store; she was actually craving a beer. On the walk home she saw Chino in front of her building and waved hello. Chino, realizing who it was, replied "what's up, snow ball?" There were a few items she needed and thought back to their earlier conversation. Could he really get anything she wanted if she had the cash? She wasn't sure how to start a conversation that could lead into her asking for the items she needed. Standing there facing him, she thought he might be the best source for procuring special items. If so, it meant she didn't have to risk the exposure of trying to locate them in person. She thought, just ask him. What was the worst that could happen, he'd go to the police? She felt comfortable that wouldn't happen.

He could tell she was thinking and the silence was beginning to thicken. He looked at her, smiling, and said, "Just say what's on your mind." She looked him in the eyes and asked if he meant it when he said he could get anything if a person had the money. Still smiling, he said "I told you, if you want it I can get it." Reluctantly, she said she had a need for a several special items that might not be on his limited menu. He told her he didn't have a menu, he was more like a buffet. If you're going to trust me, you have to start sometime. He was right. She said she needed some Thallium expecting him to have no idea what she was talking about. He didn't miss a beat. "Do you have a rat problem?", he asked. She was actually the one that was stumped. Just for his amusement, he couldn't help letting her stand there bewildered for a minute. "Rats," he repeated. "Thallium is a poison used to kill rats. That is what you want it for, right?" For a second, she wondered if he was using some hidden innuendo; did he mean people when he said rats? He laughed and told her to keep up. He said,

"Thallium is used in rat poison." She asked if that was true and he replied "Yep." Maybe he didn't know what she needed it for. Yep, rats. With his statement a new idea popped into the back of Morana's head. I have a bad rat problem she said. He said Thallium didn't come cheap but if she had the money he had the product. She felt relieved and a little more comfortable so she asked if he could get Prussian Blue. When he asked if she wanted to kill them or bring them back to life, she felt confident he know what they were for, and that it wasn't rats. She smiled and said "Both, can you get them?" He said, "That don't come cheap, but give me three days and I'll have enough for you to kill several rats."

She reached into her pocket to get money and he grinned and said, "I trust you, Prada." She thanked him and told him to have a good night. As she was turning to walk off, he said he already had a good night, she just paid his power bill. Walking into her building, she couldn't help wondering why he didn't use some kind of street slang, just proper English.

She had ordered the trunk with a prepaid debit card along with a prepaid cell phone she had purchased. It had come overnight delivery and as a precaution, she met the delivery person at the entrance of the building. The trunk was a little heavier than she had expected. As she was trying to figure out the best way to get it up to her apartment she saw Chino standing on the corner across from her building. Before she could ask him for help, he had already started walking towards her. Watching him cross the street, she couldn't help thinking that underneath his drug dealer persona and 250 pounds of scarred, tattooed muscle, he was really a decent guy. He helped her carry the trunk to the elevator where she told him she could make it the rest of the way. For some strange reason ,she felt she could trust him but wasn't willing to take the chance. Morana would never take a chance, would never make a mistake. He looked at her and knew she was doing something she wanted no one to know about. She could see in his face he knew. When he asked if she knew what she was doing, she didn't answer. As he began walking away from the elevator, he looked back and reminded her; if she had the cash, he had what she needed.

The trunk was in clear sight in her bedroom. David had no idea she had walked right by him with his coffin. She didn't know which to tell him first. Should she tell him he was going to get what he had come for, he was going to spend the night with her? Or about the special thing in her bedroom she had ordered just for him?

She looked at David, happy he was in pain. She grabbed a piece of the sandpaper, enjoying the look of fear in Davis's eyes as she picked it up. She sanded the chest in spots, primarily on the top; she wanted it to look old and used. She took a small, serrated kitchen knife she had brought from Beth's high-end Manhattan apartment and cut several deep scratches into the wood for good measure. Once she was comfortable with her work on the chest, she left it where David would be able so see it through the mirror's reflection. She was hungry; Kung Pao Chicken and an egg roll sounded good.

20 - ALL DATES END

She was curious as to whether or not she'd be nervous. She didn't know if she would be able to do it. She knew it was too risky to end "dates" the way she ended Brian's. She was confident Brian was dead but she hadn't actually killed him, she left that up to the cliff and the Ohio River. She knew it was a risk leaving a date alive when she disposed of them, no matter how effective her method. Morana couldn't make a mistake; it was a risk she wasn't willing to take.

She walked back into the room and took a minute to watch HungDavid's eyes fill with panic. She hated him. Her first high school boyfriend popped into her head. She had fallen head over heels for a boy named Neil. They dated several months her sophomore year before it ended badly. He played sports and hung out with the popular group in school. He was the popular kid. She was a brain and didn't hang out with the jocks, cheerleaders, or rich kids. She felt proud of herself for a second. She was confident she made more money than any three of them combined. Her thoughts went back to Neil. She had caught him with a cheerleader after a Friday night football game. She told him she wasn't going to be able to make it to the game. She had plans of showing up and surprising him. She definitely surprised him and he surprised her right back. From that day forward, she never felt good enough for any man she dated. It didn't matter how many men worked under her or how many men she outsmarted or out negotiated. She felt men would take any opportunity to be with someone new or different or better, perhaps by cheating on her, perhaps by cheating with her. When it came to men, she never saw herself as the someone better. To her, men never saw her as the someone better. She felt they saw her as someone different or new that could be used. Her ideology was changing. She was beginning to hate men, and she was becoming very confident.

David was about to pay for his intent to use her. She thought about Jon again and became enraged. It was time.

She knew she was going to be able to do it. She wasn't nervous, she wasn't nervous at all; in fact she felt a sense of eagerness. The nervousness she had expected was replaced by a desire, an intense desire. She was ready to end the date.

She looked at him and asked if he liked to tell his friends about his conquests. In her head, she could hear him talking about how he went into the city, added another trophy to his collection, and got away with it scot free. She was sure he would go into vivid detail about everything from the size of her breast to what she did to him and let him do to her. He probably had a rating scale. She looked at him asked if he rated women that weren't his wife. She asked where she had fallen on his scale. She leaned over towards him and looked into his eyes. She asked him where she had fallen on his scale in the "things she did to me" category. He realized her questions were asked in the past tense.

She walked out of the room and came back with a towel. Looking at him, she walked over the kitchen counter and opened a cabinet door. He could see she had two plastic bottles, each filled a third of the way with a clear liquid. She also took out a glass jar and sat all three on the countertop. She put the rubber gloves on and walked back to the bed. She could see the panic racing in every ounce of his body. He couldn't stand more acid. His testicles felt dissolved and his forehead felt as if it was on fire. She told him she wasn't going to hurt his legs anymore. She wasn't going to burn his chest or hands or groin anymore. She was done with the hammer and had put the acids away. He started to feel a glimpse of hope there was a chance she was going to let him go. Hope quickly returned to fear when she said she had put the acids away. He started to panic, wondering what she had on the kitchen counter top.

She made sure he could see she had put her gloves back on. She also made sure HungDavid could see her pull the mask out of one of the cabinets. She asked if he knew how to make gas. She told him it was very simple. Looking at him to watch his eyes, she said the simplest of all was her version of chlorine gas. She picked up one of the plastic bottles and poured the content into the glass jar. She said, "All we need is a little ammonia and a little chlorine." She lifted up the second plastic bottle and said, "Ammonia". She put her hand around the jar and said, "Chlorine". She mixed the two together and let it sit for a few seconds. She wondered if she would be able to smell the mixture through the mask. She took the jar and poured the gas onto the towel.

She could tell by watching him gasp for air the fumes were stronger than she had expected, she had to hurry. She walked over to him and released the strap that secured his forehead. She told him to lift his head up. He buried his head as deep into the mattress as he could. She asked him and again he refused. She grabbed the duct tape wrapped around his head and lifted it until his chin was resting on his chest. She wrapped the towel around the back of his head. She looked into his eyes; she wanted to enjoy one last moment of psychological torture. She slowly covered his face with the towel. As the towel covered his eyes, she thanked him for their date.

She watched David for a few minutes, long enough to see him stop jerking. Once she was satisfied he was dead she opened the den window, hoping the fan was blowing the fumes out of the apartment. She took the towel and laid it on the bathtub, then turned the shower on. She walked to the door and took a small breath to be sure the air was safe to breath. She was relieved to see the fan had worked, the air was clear. She sat the gas mask behind the door and walked out into the corridor.

She went to the first floor of her building. As she walked onto the street, she was almost amazed at how she felt; no remorse. In fact, the only feeling she had was hunger. She was so surprised, it wasn't what she'd expected She had killed for the first time. She had been anxious when she met David. She knew he wouldn't survive their date, but thought she would need to do it quickly. She didn't know if she would be able to actually kill a man. She had been concerned. Would doing it slowly give her too much time to think? She didn't want to let any conscience she may have left prevent her from finishing. Did she have any conscious left? She realized as she wrapped the towel around David's head, that the answer was no. She realized she didn't need to worry about killing quickly; she could have taken hours. She was surprised how killing these horrible men, these cheating, lying men, came so very easily for her. She knew she wouldn't need to rush with her next date.

21 - LUNCH WITH A DRUG DEALER

Now debating between her egg roll or a burger, she walked out of her building. Burger it was. She turned to head towards Bareburger on 31st Avenue and noticed Chino still on the corner; he was always on the corner. She walked up to him and asked if he ever took a day off. In his usual charming way he replied and said he had to work overtime if he was going to be rich like her. She laughed; he always seemed to make her laugh. Still smiling, she said "You go to school, you work overtime, and you take care of your brother. Do you eat or is there no time for that luxury?' He said he ate and she asked if he wanted to go grab a burger with her. He said he didn't normally date white girls, but he would make an exception for her. She said she didn't normally date drug dealers, but would make an exception for him. Ouch, he said, and they started walking.

As they walked into the restaurant,

she was a little surprised, and impressed, when he opened the door for her. They sat and she started looking over the menu. Normally, it would have been a salad, maybe a multigrain chicken club or turkey burger if she was throwing caution to the wind. Not today. Today, Beth wasn't ordering. She wanted something big, greasy, and delicious. She told Chino not to hold back; today, it was her treat. He ordered the Big Blue Bacon Burger. She said make that two with extra big on mine. They started talking. She wanted to know more about the smart, funny scholar slash drug dealer. She asked him how much money he made, and he asked her how much she made. She couldn't tell him the truth so replied, 'Enough to buy your burger!" and quickly moved to another topic.

She asked what kind of people he hung out with. She actually did want to have lunch with him, but also had a hidden agenda. He told her the type of people he hung out with was very different than the type of people she associated with. He said, For example: I hang out with people, you associate with people." She asked him if he'd ever seen anyone shot or stabbed. He told her he had been stabbed twice and had been shot at several times, but by the grace of God never hit. Hmm; a scholarly, religious drug dealer. How would he surprise her next?

She knew he was able to get any drug she wanted, and some she had probably never heard of but wanted to know if he dealt in other things. She didn't want to come right out and ask if he could get weapons, so she thought it would be better to work her way up to that question. She asked if he could get fake IDs or stolen credit card numbers. A look of concern came over his face. He asked why she wanted to know if he could get these things. He said he had seen her clothes and knew she could get her own credit cards then asked why she wanted to know if he could get fake id's. She said she was just curious and not to worry, she wasn't a rat. He smiled, she asked what was so funny. He told her she didn't look like a rat and said ID's and credit cards fall under the category 'anything you want, I can get'. She asked if he could get guns. He asked what kind of gun she wanted and why she needed a gun. She said she wanted a bazooka and said she wanted to blow up her ex-boyfriend. He knew she was making a joke, but didn't answer the question. She said since he didn't answer she would take that as a yes. Anything she wanted, right?

He looked at the waiter who was bringing their food and said yes. As they were about to dig into their big blue burgers, she said she had another question. He looked at her, waiting to hear what it was going to be this time. Then, after a few seconds of silence, asked what she wanted. Did she want him to get her a nuclear bomb or maybe a time machine? She said, "If you can get any drug I want or any weapon I want, do you know people who could do anything I want?"

He picked up his burger and said "I told you I know some bad people, but before I do anything else, for you would have to tell me what was going on."

"Just curious," she said. He looked at her with a serious face and said "You want drugs, now you ask about guns and people who will do "things". I've told you enough times, if you have the money I can get anything you want. I'll take care of your Thallium and Prussian Blues, but I have to know what is going on before I'll do anything else for you. She looked at him and he could see the look of concern on her face. She smiled through the concerned look and said, "Let's just enjoy the rest of our burgers, I may even spring for a couple of hot fudge sundaes for dessert."

As she was about to walk back into her building, she told him thanks for a date she actually enjoyed. She paused for a second then with a serious, almost vulnerable look, asked if she could trust him. He returned the serious look and said, "If I can trust you".

With that she entered her building and headed to her floor. She opened the door to her apartment and walked into the kitchen, where the smell of gas was still a little stronger than she had expected. The January air was cold, but she had to get the gas fumes out. She walked back to the door put her mask back on and walked to the bed. She removed the towel and he looked at David's face; he was dead. The skin on his face was red and his eyes were shut. Still no emotion, no regret, no guilt.

She walked over to her new trunk, placed it on rollers, and slid it to the side of the bed. She loosened his restraints and pulled his lifeless body to the side of the bed. She attempted to push his head and upper body into the trunk, but his whole body slid off the bed. His upper body landed in the trunk, but his midsection down landed arched over onto the floor. As she struggled to lift David's lower body into the trunk, she thought back to lifting Brian's body into her car and how much easier it was. When she bought the trunk, she didn't know if it would be large enough to hold a grown man's body. Fortunately, she had purchased one with a domed top, as it turned out she needed the room to allow for David's knees and head. After a struggle, she managed to get David's body in the trunk, then closed it and secured the clasp with a padlock. Tomorrow, she would call the small, local moving company where she'd rented two units.

22 - LUCKY

She had chosen the small moving company as opposed to a large chain company for two reasons. First, more anonymity in their storage unit., More importantly, she knew there would be less identification and paperwork needed. Plain Jane looking Morana had been to the unit several times. The first time, she simply walked by the place to take note of the layout and look for any surveillance or monitoring . The second time, she rented her first unit. She assumed the name of a woman she found in the obituaries and substituted her lack of ID with her uncanny ability to flirt. She had great timing in arriving at their office. She seemed to have great timing in most situations, a trait learned from Beth's real job.

The young guy at the office didn't stand a chance. She was able to talk her way into renting a unit with almost no effort. She had barely finished asking the guy behind the counter for a unit when he asked how large. His name tag read 'Lucky'; how ironic. He was young, short, and had a bad case of acne. Beth would have flirted a little and felt sincere compassion for the poor guy. Morana was torn; she almost felt sorry for him. She assumed he was a virgin, which meant he probably hadn't used or lied to any woman, at least none other than small lies trying to make himself seem better than he actually was. He probably had to do that so she didn't resent him for it.

Since she had already walked by the place, she knew the layout and the unit she wanted. She had walked around the parking lot and both sides of the building, but saw no cameras monitoring the units themselves. She had already noticed a surveillance camera focused on the front parking lot and spotted a second camera monitoring the office when she walked in the door. There was a gate around the place, which she assumed the family owners hoped would keep out thugs or angry renters who had forfeited their possessions after falling behind on rent. It appeared they couldn't afford much in the way of security and had grown complacent with the gate and front video monitoring.

There were three rows of storage building. All the units were front facing so she didn't have to worry about someone approaching the backside of the row in front of hers. She rented the second unit in the back corner of the third row.

She has purposely rented the second unit from the end to remain just out of sight from anyone entering the first two rows from the side. She rented it monthly and paid upfront through March in cash. Lucky gave her two keys, one for the gate and one for her unit. In what was basically a question, he said he would walk her to the unit. As they walked, she looked for any additional form of security or surveillance she may have missed. She looked at Lucky and, with a very vulnerable smile, asked how she could be sure her possessions would be safe, other than by him protecting them, of course.

It wasn't fair; Lucky was already putty in her hands. When she insinuated he would be protecting her, she could have asked him for the keys to the place and the combination to the safe and he would have handed both over with a set of directions.

Lucky told her they used to have a guard dog but he had gotten old and overweight and was now his roommate. Said the only thing he guarded now was his couch. He stated the obvious in telling her about the surveillance in the front and the gate around the units. That was what she had hoped to hear. With her flirtatious smile, she said if it's good enough for you, it's good enough for me.

There was no need to be indiscriminate, so she pressed for security information by asking if the units were ever robbed. She asked how long it would take the police to arrive. Lucky told her it was rare that anyone tried to rob or even get into the place. He said there was a key to the gate and a separate key to the unit, so stealing anything was hard. If someone did get in without a gate key, they'd have a tough time getting anything heavy over the gate. He said most of the people who lost their stuff had either gone to prison, gone to heaven, or simply moved and planned to retrieve it later, but never got around to it. She asked how they knew if a person had died or gone to prison. He kind of chuckled and said he never heard from the dead ones. He said those that had been locked up usually came in with a threat or sob story asking for their stuff back.

She didn't want to seem overly interested, so she changed the subject for a few minutes. She asked him if he had a girlfriend or if he was waiting on a supermodel that had just won the lottery. As they started heading back to the office, he explained there were several girls in his school who liked him, but he wasn't sure which one he wanted. One of those little white lies, she did feel sorry for him.

As she was about to walk out of the office, she thanked him then turned and asked what they did with the dead people's stuff. He had described it as stuff and she wanted to stay in his comfort area. He said they either keep it or, if it wasn't claimed after the 90 day grace period, sold it for back rent. He said they just hauled it off to the dump if it wasn't worth anything. Flirting, She asked Lucky his work hours so she could always come when he was there.

24 - THE SECOND STORAGE UNIT

On her third visit to the storage office, she had purposely gone when Lucky wasn't working. She wore a baseball cap and had sown reflective pins into the top. She pulled the bill pulled low on her forehead. She had a scarf wrapped around her neck. She wore a big coat to hide her figure, jeans, and shoes she had bought from a discount store. Thanks to her first meeting with Chino, this time she remembered Prada stood out. The guy working today wasn't as easy as Lucky, but she explained she had rented in the past and explained all she had to do to get the unit. The guy behind the counter was Tony and he wanted a driver's license. Luckily, he was willing to take money instead. He told her he might be able to overlook the license if she had the "no identification fee". She acted upset but paid his small storage unit extortion fee. The second unit she rented was two down from the first. She had asked Lucky if it was available before she rented the first one. Again, she paid cash for the first three months rent. Tony didn't offer to give the tour. She told him she didn't need to store anything now, but would come back later. He had his money and was happy to see her leave after he gave her the keys.

She had filled several small boxes with clothes and miscellaneous items she'd purchased from the discount store where she now did her personal shopping. She let an hour pass, then drove back while Tony was still there. She wasn't concerned about Lucky but wanted to see what typical protocol was when someone needed to get to their unit. He barely acknowledged her as she walked through the gate. She acted like she was having a little trouble with the boxes to see if he would help. He didn't. She had hoped he wouldn't. The less interaction she had to have with the employees, the better.

She put the boxes in the unit and made another check for any security she may have overlooked on her previous trips. She had made it a point to rent units that were out of site of the office and not visible from any roads. Once she was satisfied with lack of visibility, and lack of surveillance, she left.

24 - JUNK IN THE TRUNK

When the movers knocked on the door, she went to the bathroom and turned the shower on. With a raised voice, she told them the door was open. When they were in the apartment, she explained she was in the shower. She told them her unit number and that the chest was all she needed moved. She had left the money on the chest and told them she had included a tip. They counted the money and pocketed their tip. They took the chest and closed the door behind them without seeing her.

Her "date" was over, as was her weekend. She headed back to Beth's apartment in the city to get some sleep. She needed to rest to get ready for another week of Beth's boring job, a job that used to be exciting. A job that used to keep her adrenaline flowing. The job that used to make her feel a little 'holier than thou' was now so mundane she counted the minutes until Friday. Getting into bed, she began to wonder again if she would feel guilt or remorse, but she was asleep before she could finish the thought.

25- LUCKYLOTTO

It was Thursday night, and she had read through countless emails from men hoping to meet Morana. She could tell by the content most seemed to be lonely or boring. The replies that didn't fall into one of those categories seem to just be horny. There was no new stand out emails from men who seemed to meet her specific criteria.

It was almost 11:00 and she was

about to log out and get ready for another day of Beth's now painfully ordinary job when she received a second email from the Lottery Guy.

His screen name was luckylotto2. His first email simply read "I just won the lottery and would love to meet you". She had become better at deciphering the intent of the emails but to her this one was intriguing. With no other content, she wasn't able to get a feel for the guy's true intentions. He had peaked her interest. After receiving his first email, she viewed his profile and saw he was handsome, or at least the picture he had posted was of a handsome man. He described himself as single, well built and athletic, they all did. She opened the second email, which read "I did win the lottery and I do want you. She decided not to reply tonight, but Luckylotto2 would soon find out how unlucky he was.

26 - LOTTO'S FIRST EMAIL

Beth left the office early on Friday and got an order of sweet and sour pork along with two egg rolls from her favorite Chinese restaurant on 8th Avenue. She was excited her week was finally over and couldn't wait to get home. She didn't know which she was more eager to do, dive into her egg rolls or log into Morana's account; the egg rolls won.

It had been a boring week, both at work and in her quest for finding her next Mr. Right. Finishing her first egg roll, she logged in to respond to the lotto guy and noticed he had emailed her again. It was as short as the first. It read "Hello, the lottery guy again. Please respond". Eager to avoid a boring weekend stuck as Beth, she replied. Not willing to be the first to start any real conversation, she kept her response short. Her reply read "Hi lotto2, why the number two?"

She had decided to call him lotto instead of Lucky. Lucky was her storage unit guy, and even though she had begun to hate men, she couldn't help finding a soft spot in her heart for him.

Lotto replied almost immediately. She noticed his second request came at 9:11 pm, the others had come closer to midnight. Of course he hadn't won the lottery and she debated making him dance in circles from the beginning. She wanted to reply asking why a lottery winner couldn't find better things to do than spend all of his time on front of a computer. She wanted to ask how boring his life really was, then couldn't help but smile as she realized Morana was online every night and her life was anything but boring.

His initial emails had been very short, but not this one. He seemed eager to talk. It was all too apparent he both enjoyed talking about himself and wanted to impress her.

He started the email with the fact that he had won the mega millions lottery twice. He said he hadn't won the big lotto but had won a million dollars twice, both times having five numbers and a 5x's multiplier. Of course he was lying, and liars had something to hide. He had potential.

She wanted to appease him to find out all she could about this lotto liar. She asked him to open and instant chat, which he did immediately. She said he had to be very happy and must be the kind of guy people wanted to be around. She knew men all too well, if she showed interest and showered him with compliments they were more than willing to talk about themselves. He was. He typed she better believe he was happy but that he had to be super selective about the people he hung out with. He didn't want anybody to try using him for his money. He said he acted like he didn't have none so nobody would try to get any from him. He gave himself away too easily. She read the words "super" and "hung out" then counted the times he used double negatives. Not only was he lying and uneducated, she was confident his profile picture was about as real as his lottery money. Now she wanted to meet this guy.

She said she understood how he must be worried about people trying to take advantage of him. Said she really hated when a person tried to take advantage of her. She asked why he was on this site trying to meet women, he must have plenty of girls chasing him and had to be a great catch. The more she said, the more confidant he seemed to become. She knew the more confidant he became, the more lies he would tell. She was eager to keep their conversation going and see how many times he talked himself into a corner. If he turned out to be the kind of "date" she was looking for, not only was he going to meet her qualifications, he was going to be fun.

He said he set up the dating site so he could meet girls who didn't know about his money. He wanted to find a good girl, he didn't want no gold digger. She told him she understood. She wanted to ask why his intro to their first conversation regarded his new found wealth if he wanted so badly to keep it concealed. He was too easy. She wanted to lure him in a little more. Besides, she thought, that sentence may be a little past his grade level.

She confirmed she was a "good girl" and stroked his ego at the same time by telling him she answered his ad without knowing anything about the money. He asked if it was just because of his picture. How dumb could this guy be? It almost wasn't fair to him, he was so much lower than her on the pay scale of life. Not only did he actually believe someone who said they didn't respond because of his money, Lotto was in his name, and he didn't even realize he was giving his fake profile picture away. She knew he was already worried she wouldn't like his true looks. Poor Lotto lacked confidence. Money and fake picture, he was trying to overcompensate for something. He abruptly stopped emailing.

She sent him an email and waited for a response, but he was offline. She wondered why the abrupt stop. He lied about his picture, he lied about his money, and of course he was lying about women. It was obvious he was no ladies' man, but she was now growing more confident that perhaps he was in a relationship, maybe even a marriage.

26 - THE TRANSITION

She liked Morana better. Saturday morning, she walked into Morana's apartment and immediately plugged in her laptop. She was online and in her profile before she took her coat off. Her new hobby was becoming an addiction. She thought about it constantly. Her mood soured when she was online and found no new prospective dates attempting to be manipulative or adulterous.

She was disappointed to see no new emails from lotto. She became even more disappointed thinking about how empty her weekend was beginning to look.

A normal Saturday consisted of shopping for overpriced clothes, followed by meet co-workers out for an overpriced dinner before going back to her overpriced apartment. Sunday would be a day full of spa treatments, hair salons and an appointment with her always booked mani/pedi girl. She would end the day of spoiling herself with expensive wine, dinner and dessert at her favorite snooty restaurant; where she would be accompanied by the painful realization of how lonely she was.

She wasn't in her lonely apartment, she was in Morana's apartment and she wasn't going to waste another weekend feeling pity for herself or wallowing in her loneliness. Morana had no intention of repeating Beth's boring, monotonous, one weekend closer to wasting her life routine. She enjoyed very different weekend activities now, and she was going to find a way to fill her Saturday with just those kinds of activities.

She began searching through profiles of men. She was looking for those that just looked like liars or jerks or cheaters. She laughed out loud when she thought to herself how they all matched that profile. She had narrowed her search down to two and was penning an email to some guy named hammy85 when she realized what she was doing. She deleted the email and logged out of her account.

Morana's intent was to show men the

error of their ways when they attempted to cheat or manipulate those who love them. She was about to search out men and tempt them into activities that may be outside of their character. She realized if she began to search for men who, to her knowledge, had done nothing wrong, her actions would be the same as those men who searched out innocent women. She had quickly grown to dislike men in general but was looking for a particular type of man. If she went online and lured someone they wouldn't truly meet her criteria. An idea popped into her head.

27 - THE SECOND DATE.

She put her coat and gloves back on, locked her apartment door, and headed towards the lobby of her building. She hopped he would be there and smiled when she saw him. She was going to go on a different date of sorts. As she walked towards him, she was a little perplexed. She hated men, but for some reason, really enjoyed Chino's company. She also felt so sorry for Lucky that she would have probably said yes if he had asked her out. She knew the latter would never happen; Lucky was a sweet guy, but wouldn't grow the balls to ask a woman like her out in two lifetimes.

He smiled back as she approached him. She got within earshot and said she thought gangsters didn't smile. She thought they were all hard. That all they did was beat people up 24 hours a day, when they weren't looting and pillaging that was. He didn't miss a beat. He said he thought rich girls who wore Prada and Louis Vuitton lived in Manhattan and didn't hang out with drug dealers, no matter how good looking they were.

She didn't realize it until it was too late. She hugged him hello. She was as startled as he was when she realized she was doing it. She quickly pulled away and apologized. All at once, a bunch of thoughts raced through her head. She wondered if she hugged him because she felt sorry for him leading such a tough life. Maybe it was because he was taking care of his brother with no parents and still went to school. Maybe it was just the fact that he was a drug dealer but didn't want to be. As of late, she could appreciate going to a job you hated day after day. She also couldn't believe she had just admitted to herself she hated her job. Her precious, prestigious job that so many people would love to have but so few did, especially women.

She was a little embarrassed. She had gone from hugging him to pensive thought all in a matter of seconds. She was relieved when he laughed off her apology and said not to worry about it, all the ladies like Chino. She didn't want to admit it but he was probably right, all the ladies just might like Chino. She realized that for just a second something was happening, something that she made it a point to never let happen. Chino was steering the relationship. She had to get herself together.

Shaking off the embarrassing hug followed by the deep thought, which she was sure evoked a staring into space image, she regained her composure. After all who didn't like a "just because I wanted to hug you" hug…especially when it came from a woman as hot as she was. That thought helped, she was herself again.

She asked Chino if he could check with his assistant to see if his calendar was free for the evening. He said he didn't need an assistant. He was CEO of Chino Enterprises and all decisions were made by him and were binding in the court of street law. Good, she said. You're taking the night off and not only are you taking the night off, you're taking me to dinner at the restaurant of my choosing. He smiled briefly until he realized she was serious. He opened his mouth to say he couldn't just not be there. Before he got two words out, she asked how many chances he'd have to go out with a girl like her. Her confidence was back. He was halfway through saying he went out with women like her all the time when he stopped mid-sentence. They both knew that wasn't true. Where do you want to go, he asked. She grabbed his shoulder and turned him away from their building while acting as if she was thinking. As they walked towards Queens Boulevard, she told him she was just kidding about the place of her choice. After all, it was the man's responsibility to pick the restaurant and she wanted to find a new joint that came highly recommended by Chino himself. He looked at her and said "The man's responsibility huh Ok, as long as you remember what the women's responsibility is." "Of course," she said. "Pick dessert." He said he knew just the place as long as she promised not to drink a bunch of 40oz and embarrass him.

As they walk up Queens Blvd, joking and trying not to miss an opportunity to make fun of each other, Chino stopped and looked at her with an almost scary sincerity. She felt her heart begin to race; did he know something about her, had he seen her with Brian? Had he been a cop the whole time she was talking about drugs and guns and everything else incriminating? It seemed like forever before he finally began to speak. He said, "I have a very important question to ask you and I am going to need an honest answer." It was freezing outside, but she could feel herself start to sweat. Hoping she didn't look the way she felt and trying to suppress emotion, she looked him in the face. Answer honestly, she said, I'll try. Just tell me, have you ever had pig trotter or oxtail. She was dumbfounded. What are you talking about? He said I didn't think so. It's the man's choice right, so here we are. He opened the door to a small restaurant she didn't even realize they were standing in front of and said welcome to the Salt and Fat. Speechless, she walked in.

You are going to love this place he said. I'm sure it's right up your alley. Smiling, he said, just let me do the ordering. As they were seated, she realized she could take a breath. He was only being dramatic because he was bringing her to some place with the name salt and fat in it, or was that the name? As the waiter brought the menus, and the complimentary popcorn and bacon, he said they didn't need them, they already knew what they wanted. We do, she said in the form of a question.

Looking at the waiter he said, "Yep, we're going to share an order of your finest pork belly buns and the lady will have an order of your freshest Crispy Pig Trotter. I'll be having your Oxtail Terrine. We would both like to follow that with some Avocado Ice-cream." The waiter said, "Great choices," and walked away. Once again dumbfounded, all she could say was "avocado Ice cream." He laughed and said "I just ordered pigs feet and the tail of an ox, and you're worried about eating ice cream made with avocado? If it will make you feel better I'll change our ice ream order to their Rice Krispies Marshmallow ice cream." He had done it again? She was truly surprised, maybe the most surprised yet.

After he jokingly offered her a free snow cone she, ever so slowly and reluctantly, took her first ever bite of pigs feet. She was shocked, they were really good. They finished dinner, avoiding the avocado ice cream, and headed back to her apartment. Or, as Chino liked to refer to it, Chino Enterprises National Headquarters. As they made it to her building, Chino, looking over both shoulders, said he had something for her. He pulled two sandwich bags out of one of his many pant pockets and handed them to her. At first, she didn't realize what he was giving her. Their date had been so unofficial with no serious mention of drugs or weapons or anything of the sort. As she took them, he said "I told you to give me a couple of days, it's been a couple of days." She snapped back to Morana's reality and asked how much she owed him. He told her it was $250 for both, but he would give her a 10% "willing to eat pigs feet" discount. As she opened her wallet flush with cash, he said he needed to quit his job and become a receptionist. She thanked him for such a luxurious dinner and was about to walk away when he said he saw how nervous she got earlier at the mention of a serious question and repeated he wouldn't do anything else for her if she didn't tell him what was going on. He took enough risks and trust went both ways he said, followed by his usual smile and a good night.

28 - LOTTO

She felt happy. She had a fun with Chino and considered just going to bed, but the lure was too much. She had to login. She hoped there would be a new email, a new guy a new date. Before she could even check her inbox, Lotto sent her an IM. He asked what she was doing, then asked what she was wearing. She felt happy for a different reason. Without answering, she asked why he had ended their last conversation so abruptly. She couldn't wait to hear his reply. He said my bad, said his internet just quit in the middle of an IM he had typed where he was going to tell her how hot she was and how much he liked her. He was going to ask her if she liked him. Lucky her. He was not only a brainiac, he was also the original Casanova. She replied yes, she liked him and his money didn't have nothing to do with it. Why not dumb herself down, it made it a little more fun.

She was debating which mundane question she should ask. Where did he work, what were his hobbies did he like sports. The question was unimportant, as was the answer. She just wanted to keep him talking so she could keep feeling him out. He surprised her before she had a chance to decide. He asked if they could meet. She instantly replied yes. When and where? He said she couldn't come to his house because he was staying in a hotel. He explained he was having remodeling stuff done to it with his lottery money. She didn't know if she could dumb herself down enough. He asked where she was and she replied New York. He said no way, he had been thinking about coming to The Big Apple while his house was being redone. There you go, she said, you can come see me as long as your girlfriends won't be too mad. He said he only had the one but he was going to break-up with her because she got pregnant. That was all she needed. She said she understood and asked how soon he could get to The Big Apple. He said he had to go but would be back online in a few minutes. She could visualize his pregnant girlfriend coming into the room trying to look over his shoulder, trying to see what he was up to. He was offline before she could type 'okay'.

29 - "JUSTFRIENDS"

Still sitting in front of her compute and becoming ever more furious at the thought of a man leaving his pregnant girlfriend, she received an email. The sender's profile name is "JustFriends". The email read he had come across her profile and noticed she was online. She looked like a nice girl and he wondered if she would like to talk for a while. She would typically discard this type of innocent email and block the sender's profile, but thanks to lotto's pregnant girlfriend, she hated all men at the moment. Besides, she had time to kill while she waited to see of Lotto was going to come back online. She almost hoped he didn't. She hoped he had been caught and that his girlfriend had enough sense to throw him out.

She responded to JustFriends saying sure, she was always up for good conversation. They probably had very different ideas on the types of conversations each were looking for.

He sent her an IM invite and she accepted. He said he was coming out of a relationship that wasn't going to work and wanted to talk. The word relationship caught her interest. She was typing the standard, almost expected, I'm sorry when he said he was in New York. He said people just didn't realize how difficult it was to meet someone who shares the same interests even in a city of millions. He asks if she's had ever found herself in a bad situation. She wondered why he didn't say relationship. As he was about to answer Lotto came back online. She said she couldn't talk now but said yes when he asked if he could talk to her again.

30 - MEETING LOTTO

Lotto's IM popped up and again he said my bad. He said he had to check his itinerary to see when he could make it to the city. No Big Apple this time she thought. He said he could come as soon as next week if she was available. Said he would have little free time and could only stay for the night because of his girlfriend. No problem she said thinking he must have used his time offline to think of a sentence with proper grammar. She asked if he would be flying in and if so from where. Mustang Oklahoma he replied. Sure she thought, was there even such a place. She asked if he would mind meeting her in the city, said she didn't really know her way around the airport. Of course he didn't mind.

She asked if they could meet at Queens Plaza and was a little surprised at how quickly he said yes. this guy sounded like he wouldn't be able to find the airport if he weren't flying into it.

She wanted to be close enough to make it back to her apartment quickly but far enough away that she could abandon the date if things didn't go right. He asked what time she wanted to meet even though they hadn't agreed on a day yet. Typical man, he was willing to leave his pregnant girlfriend at the drop of a dime for a chance to sleep with another woman. She didn't bother mentioning the fact he didn't know the day they were going to meet, after all he didn't seem to be the picture of intelligence. She said 4:00 on Saturday at Queens Plaza and asked if she would be able to recognize him from his profile picture. He said he had made a few changes to his looks so she might have difficulty finding him. Of course he had. She told him to meet her at the intersection of Queens Plaza and 24th street wearing an Oklahoma Sooners ball cap, red sweatshirt and neon yellow gloves. She said she would be wearing the same thing and couldn't help thinking how silly he was for believing her. She knew he would look nothing like his fictitious profile picture but the yellow gloves would make him easy to find. Saturday it was, Beth's week couldn't go by fast enough.

Her fast pace action packed job had crawled its way to an end. It was finally Saturday and she had to get ready for her big date. It was almost 2:00 when she began doing herself in the typical low fashion everyday clothes. She went with a medium brown wig, oversized grey sweatshirt and jeans two sizes too big. She wore white tennis shoes a brown barn jacket and no make-up. There, she was as plain as they come. It was almost 3:00 so she gave the apartment a quick once over to be sure all necessities were in place then headed to Queens Plaza. She wanted to be early and allow a little extra time for the longer route she planned to take when bringing Lotto back to her building.

She killed a little time walking around

and realizing the Plaza offered very little in the way of interesting sight seeing, she did like that fact it had a bikeway. She made her way to the corner of Queens Plaza N. and 24th St. and was a little surprised at how quickly she spotted a red sweatshirt accompanied by a pair of neon yellow gloves. No cap but the gloves were enough. The person was in front of her so she walked up from behind and tapped them on the shoulder. They turned around and she realized it was a woman. She apologized, said she had the wrong person and hoped the lady didn't say she was the Luckylottto2. No problem the woman said when she felt someone tap her on the shoulder. She turned her head and saw a pair of yellow gloves sliding down her arm. Luckylotto she asked and they guy replied yes. She was surprised to see he was actually good looking. He was thin but seemed in shape. He removed his cap and revealed short dark hair with almost chiseled cheekbones. She noticed his nice complexion and deep blue eyes, which almost stood out. He didn't look at all the uneducated country bumpkin she had expected. He asked how she was and still a little stunned she replied great and you. As he began

talking his voice was nothing like what she had expected and he spoke proper grammar.

He said it had been a long trip and asked if she was ok with them going back to her apartment. Right to the point, weren't they all. No wining and dining she asked. Sure but he wanted to clean himself up before he showed her a good time. Why wasn't she surprised. They grabbed a cab and headed towards 41st Street. She said it was on the corner of 48th Street. She hoped coming to her building from the back and two blocks over would make it a little more difficult to find in the event anything went wrong, and it did.

31 - LOTTO'S DATE

They arrived at her building and started walking to the elevator. As they waited for the elevator door to open she reached into her pocket to be sure the Thallium was easily accessible. She began to feel uneasy when he started staring at her. He stared a little too long then said he was sorry he just didn't think she would be so hot. There was the Lotto she expected. The door opened and as they stepped into the corridor and began walking towards her apartment she noticed him staring at her ass. Pregnant girlfriend and all he can think about is my ass. Enough she thought, she was ready to get the date started. She unlocked her door and walked in. Before both feet crossed the threshold he pushed her in and slammed the door behind him. Instantly her guard flew up and she turned to ask what he was doing. Before she could get the first word out of her mouth he began speaking. He said they both knew why he was here and he wasn't interested in wasting time. She realized his profile picture wasn't the only thing fake about this guy.

As he started moving towards her he said he had done this lots of times. I use the stupid Luckylotto profile to weed out girls. Girls willing to meet a man with a pregnant wife simply because he had a little money. His eyes grew a little more intense and he said anybody willing to meet a guy about to abandon a pregnant woman because he had money was only interested in one thing and he was only interested in one thing. She didn't panic, she never panicked. Instantly she began thinking how she could regain control of her situation. He got face to face with her and pushed her down the short hallway. He pushed so hard she fell backwards and into her den. He said he was no dumb ass. The stupid red sweatshirt and cap, the pathetic yellow gloves. She wanted to see him to be sure he was good looking. He hoped she wasn't disappointed because he definitely wasn't. He grabbed her, lifted her up then threw her down on her couch.

You have no idea where I live no idea how I got here and no idea how to find me except through the stupid fake profile I've already deleted. He saw her laptop and told her to feel free to login in. You won't find the profile and you won't find me after today. You know what's going to happen and I hope you fight, that makes it fun. He lifted her by the right arm and yanked her barn jacket off. Still standing in front of her he lifted her sweatshirt up from the back and pulled it over her head. He told her he was going to rape her and that she was going to like it. I know where you live and I will be watching you. If you even look at a policeman on the street I will come back and what I'm about to do will seem like a sweet dream compared to my next visit. He pushed her back on the couch. He pushed her so hard the two front legs came up and the couch rocked backwards almost flipping over. He stepped to his right blocking the hallway and took his sweatshirt off. He wasn't wearing a shirt underneath it and she saw he was muscular. He was strong and in shape. She wouldn't be able to fight him, she had to think quick.

All of her tools were in the kitchen and she knew she wouldn't be able to make if off the couch and across the den before he could get to her. Undressing he had given her enough time to regain her composure. In a timid voice she said she didn't believe he had deleted his profile, not if he did this before. He started taking his pants off and told her to check if she didn't believe him. She got off the couch, walked over to her small desk and sat down. Looking at him she noticed he was trying to take his pants off with his shoes still on. As quickly as she could she opened the website and pulled up the first guy's profile she saw. She looked at him and told him his profile was still up, she was looking at it now.

He looked up and started walking towards her pulling his pants up. He walked behind her left side staring at the computer screen. He saw it wasn't his profile and was about to say something when she stood up and slammed the corner of the laptop into his left temple. She tried to step over him but he lifted his leg and she stumbled and fell in front of the couch. She pushed herself up to her knees but he grabbed her left ankle. She looked back at him and kicked him with her right foot. The heel of her tennis shoe made contact with his nose and she could feel the nasal bones shatter. She ran into the kitchen, opened a cabinet and grabbed the squirt bottle filled with Muriatic Acid. She made it half way back into the den and squirted the acid all over his chest. As he began to scream and cough from the fumes she quickly went back into the kitchen. She and grabbed a hammer and took a deep breath She walked over to him and using the side of the hammer hit him in

the head knocking him unconscious.
Morana won.

She raised the window in her den and held her head out to take a breath before walking back into the kitchen. She got the gas mask from under the sink and turned the water on. She soaked a kitchen towel and wrapped it around her head then fumbled over to Lotto and put the mask over his face. She wasn't going to let gas fumes end her date early. Unsure how long he would remain unconscious she went back into the kitchen and filled a large bowl with water. She walked back to Lotto and poured it over his chest. She did it a few more times then put her gloves on and grabbed her handcuffs. She rolled Lotto unto his back and handcuffed his right wrist to his left ankle.

She poured a few more bowls of water on his chest before sitting the fan in front of him to blow the fumes out the window. As she rolled the bed into the kitchen she realized she'd never the known the kind of rage she felt towards the odious person unconscious on her den floor. Lotto will suffer.

Dragging him by the handcuffs hoping his shoulder would dislocate she got him into the kitchen. She took the wet towel and wiped his chest then rinsed it out twice. Knowing lifting him in his current position would be a challenge, she kept him on his stomach and put her knee on his neck before undoing the cuff on his ankle and putting it on his left hand. She wrapped a releasable zip tie around his ankles, rolled him over and put the wet towel on his chest. Leaning down, keeping the towel between her chest and his, she grabbed him under the arms and lifted him until his butt is sitting on the bed. She pushed his upper body onto the mattress and lifted his feet and straightened his body out on the bed. She took off his shoes and thought how nice of him it was to have almost taken his pants off for her. She took off his shoes pulled his pants off so he was naked. She used a ratchet strap with a loop around each foot before tightening the strap to secure his feet. She strapped a second around his neck. She put a piece of duct tape over his mouth and pulling his arm away as far as the strap would allow undid the handcuffs.

She didn't realize until the cuffs were undone he was regaining consciousness. He freed his right arm and grabbed her pants. He pulled her into the bed frame and tried to lean up. He was choking himself with the neck strap but didn't let go of her pants until she hit him in his broken nose. As he threw his hands up to his nose she wrapped a third strap around his chest pinning his arms under his chin and dropped under the bed to ratchet it until it was secure. When she stood up he tried to reach for her but wasn't able to lift his body, the straps were too tight.

She leaned against the kitchen counter and let him jerk until he realized he wasn't going anywhere before she began to explain what was about to happen. She said her original plan for him, when she thought he was just like any other man all too eager to commit adultery, was far too good for him now. She explained her intent had been for him to feel pain like the pain the mother of his child would feel if she know his actions and how she was being treated. That's what was going to happen. She said her plans had changed a little since he tried to rape her, since he'd raped before.

His respiratory system was clearing and between the muted coughs and the blood spraying from his nose he tried to scream. She took the hammer and slammed into his right humerus bone then cuffed his elbows together. She leaned over him and cuffed her right hand over his mouth and with her left raised the hammer. Reeling from the pain in his shoulder his eyes were begging her not to hit him again. She walked over to the counter, put the hammer down then went into the bedroom and rolled out her torture table. She picked up a staple gun and by the time he realized what was about to happen she had already begun shooting staples into the tape over his mouth. He could feel the staples hitting chin bone. She shot staples through his lips that bent on his teeth. When he tried to lift his elbows to stop her she picked the hammer up and he could feel his ulna shatter when she slammed into his left elbow. The pain from feeling the broken bone each time he tried to raise his arms he stopped. She looked down at him with a shattered shoulder, elbow and nose, his body bound and duct tape stapled to his mouth and smiled.

She said, now I have plans for you, and unlike your rape plan, you're not going to like it. She told him to get comfortable.

Said it was going to be a long night and walked out of the kitchen.

When she returned to the kitchen Lotto could see through the mirror she was dragging a large box. She pulled a small stick and a length of piano wire out of the box. She tied the piano wire into a circle and slipped it over his right hand onto his wrist. She took the stick and began using it as a garrote twisting until the wire was cutting into his skin. She looked at him and said she was going to be sure he never used that hand to hurt another woman.

She took the duct tape and tore a long piece then strapped it from one side of the bedframe over his forehead and onto the other side of the frame. She told him she wouldn't want him to miss anything with such a great view from the mirror.

She reached in the box again pulling out a rat cage and asks how he was enjoying their date so far. She sat the cage on the counter and, looking into the mirror to be sure Lotto could see her, said he looked very hungry.

She picked the hammer up from beside the cage and walked to the end of the bed. She asked how he liked walking over woman and slammed the hammer into the ball of his right foot. As she saw the pain shooting thru his body she picked up a nail and tried to hold it to the ball of his left foot. He wiggled his foot and the nail slipped out of place. She told him he wasn't cooperating and she knew how much he liked it when his dates didn't cooperate. When women fight it makes it more fun for you right? She smiled and said it makes it more fun for me too then lowered the hammer on his right ankle just hard enough to get his attention. She picked the nail back up and shoved it into the ball of his foot then slammed it with the hammer. She saw the nail sticking out of his foot as she walked away from the bottom of the bed. She smiled at him and said just for good measure then slammed the hammer on the ball of his foot again. Almost laughing she walked away from bed asking if he thought he would be able to walk over people now.

She noticed he was crying and said don't worry, I am going to help you forget all about the pain in your feet. She picked up a small piece of wood lying in the corner of the kitchen and pulled out a hand held drill. She taped two forks together and wedged them between his lower legs with the prongs jabbing into the shin bone and calf muscle of each. She took a strap and tightened it at his knees. She got onto the bed and sat over his legs. She asked if he had hoped she would be straddling him tonight. She pulled a two inch screw out of the box and drilled into the wood until it was secure then sat the wood on his left shin. Forcefully leaning down on the wood she pushed the trigger and screwed through the wood until she hit bone then stopped. She looked him in the eyes and said rape hurts tell me when this does and pulled the trigger again screwing until she felt the bone cracking. She kept the trigger engaged until she felt the screw go thru his tibia. He passed out.

She walked away from the bed and went to check on her laptop. She had put a lot of time and software into the computer and wanted to see if she had broken it in the fight. She was relieved to find the only thing wrong was the lid didn't lie flush with the base. She turned it on and the screen worked. More importantly she was able to connect to the internet. She wanted to see if she had any emails from potential dates but was more interested in "JustFriends" and hoped he had emailed. He had and was online. She responded to his email and got an offer to IM from him. She accepted the IM and he asked what she was up to tonight. She wondered what his reaction would be if she told him she had a man bound to a bed in her kitchen and was torturing him. Would he believe her? She replied, just another boring night and asked how he was. He said a little sad, the nights seemed longer now and he wished he had something exciting to do. Thinking about how much she was enjoying the excitement of her evening she replied, who knows, maybe you will soon.

He asked if they could talk for a while, maybe make both their nights a little less boring. Why not she said, Lotto was passed out and definitely not going anywhere. He said he was in pharmaceutical sales and lived in Queens. She didn't know if she believed him but knew she hadn't mentioned she lived in Queens. What a small world she thought, if he was being honest. How could she find out? Who knew, they might be neighbors. So far he seemed innocent enough. She wanted him to keep talking, she didn't know if he was her type. She asked how his relationship ended and did they still see each other. He said he had ended it because he found her with another man doing things to him she shouldn't have been doing. She asked what kind of things and he simply said things she would regret. He told her he was a nice guy and thought before him she had probably hurt other men. Usually by now she would have ended this type of conversation. He didn't seem like the type of man she was in search of but for some reason she wanted to keep talking to him. She could hear Lotto, he was regaining consciousness. She said she had to go but asked if he would be around tomorrow. He said he was always around and she could talk to him anytime. She closed the IM and walked back into the kitchen.

She wanted Lotto awake and aware so she rubbed smelling salt under his nose. The pain woke him and, looking at her, he was again aware of where he was and what was happening. She congratulated him for regaining consciousness, said he was truly a tough guy. She looked at the rat cage and said now let's' get back to our fun evening. She took a pot from under the sink and poured a small amount of cooking oil into it and turned the burner on high. Picking up the duct tape she walked back to the bed and told him it was vital he lie still. She wrapped the tape around his forehead several more times until she was sure he couldn't move. When she was comfortable the strap around his neck and the tape had his head virtually immobile she took a piece of plastic tube out of the rat cage with her right hand and with her left picked the rat up by his tail. She placed the tubing over his right eye, and said this will help you see the error of your ways as she dropped the mouse into the opening head first. Petrified he tried to move his head but couldn't. As tightly as the tube allowed he forced his eye shut. She watched as the rat bit through his eyelid and into his eye. She held the tube in place long enough for it to destroy his eye then slid it from his face onto a plate trapping the rat until she dropped it back into the cage. In his left eye there was a terror she hadn't seen in either of her previous dates. She realized the horrific person Morana was becoming, she had no intention of stopping.

She let Lotto lay there for a few minutes and considered ending the date. Not yet she thought, he had been violent, he deserved to suffer. She noticed she had salt packets on her counter left over from carry out she had ordered. She opened one of the packets and poured the salt into what remained of his eye. She asked if he wanted her to rinse the salt from his eye. She could hear him try to mumble and said I'll take that as a yes. She turned and got the grease from the stove and slowly dripped some it into what was essentially his mutilated eye. Now she was ready to end the date.

She took her pipe and straddled him purposely hitting the wood in his leg. She shoved the pipe under his back and lifted. Her weight kept his midsection down and the chest strap kept his upper body secure. She lifted until she heard his spine crack the got off of him and looked at his mutilated body admiring her work.

She needed him unconscious. She took the thallium from her pocket and dissolved in a small glass of water. She cut a small hole in the tape covering his mouth and slowly poured the drink into his mouth. She waited until the drug had taken effect and walked out of the kitchen into her bedroom.

She took the wheelchair out of the closet and rolled it into the den. She walked back to Lotto removed the garrote and the strap over his chest then removed the board from his legs. She shoved his left arm as far behind his back as the strap around his leg and the tape over his forehead allowed then shoved his left arm under his back. She lifted his right side as much as she could then pushed his right arm behind his back cuffing his wrist together. She wished she could have left him awake so he could feel the pain in his shoulder and elbow. Once his arms were secure she removed the straps and cut his head free from the tape. She rolled the wheelchair backwards as close to the bed as she could and locked the wheels. Lifting under his arms she pulled him off the bed and into the chair. He was handcuffed, unconscious and she thought paralyzed below the waist but to avoid any unexpected problem she zip tied his ankles together. She was confident he wasn't going anywhere. She walked into the bathroom and started filling the tub. She let the water run until the tub was half full then went to get Lotto, is was time.

She pushed the chair into the bathroom facing the tub and locked the wheels she had already dissolved the Prussian Blues into another glass of water.

She ripped the tape from his mouth then poured the drink slowly into a funnel. Once she had poured the entire glass down his throat she put another piece of tape over his mouth. She stood beside the tub and waited for the Blues to revive him. Still hazy he regained consciousness and slowly began to realize she was sitting in front of a tub full of water. He tried to jerk forward to free himself from the chair. Using the momentum of his upper body she pushed him forward out of the chair into the tub. He fell face first into the water with his legs hanging out. She kicked the chair out of her way and pushed his legs over the side into the back of the tub. To no avail he began trying to lift his head out of the water. It was pointless, all he could do was breathe the water into his shattered nose. She liked watching as his body jerked. She drained the tub, it was time to get rid of Lotto.

On one of her many trips to the public library she was surprised to learn how easily a body could be liquefied. You need lye and hot water, she had both. She removed the cuffs and tape from Lotto then began boiling water. It took four big pots and most of the night to boil enough water to do the job. She opened the window and placed a system of fans blowing out of the den window to rid the apartment of fumes. She had several hours to kill so she called a cab bundled up and left the apartment.

32 - THE BREAK-UP

She wasn't going to spend the next four hours walking the streets of Queens, so she decided to go back to Beth's for the night. As she walked out of her apartment, she saw Chino, he really did work all the time. She thought about walking up to him placing her finger to his back telling him to give her all his money but decided the risk of getting beat up for the second time tonight wasn't worth it. With a raised voice, she said Salt and Fat, he turned, saw her and replied snowball. She asked if he could take another night off. He said you do know you're in Queens on a Saturday night right. He had a point. He asked what she was doing out this late by herself. Said someone would take her fancy Gucci wallet before she made it to the next block. She chuckled thinking if he only knew what was in her tub. He asked what was so funny and she said she had him to protect her.

No romantic date tonight he said, I've got to make rent. She said, speaking of romantic nights don't you have time for a girlfriend or does Chino Enterprises keep you to busy? He smiled at her and said he was going to ask her to be his girlfriend but knew he couldn't compete with a receptionist salary. Besides, we're just friends and I wouldn't want hanky panky to mess that up. She said since you didn't get me flowers could you at least talk to me until my cab gets here. As he was saying he could do that her cab pulled up. She told him good night and for just a second actually thought about hugging him again. As she climbed into the cab he said you never did tell me what you were doing.

She got back to Morana's apartment early Sunday morning. She hadn't slept, she was too excited to get back to her tub. When she walked into her bathroom, she saw that the lye had done exactly what she had hoped it would do. She knew lye was just a stronger version of Drano and was safe to drain into her tub. She put the mask and a rubber glove on and lifted the bathtub stopper with a coat hanger. She had brought a metal strainer and a brick she had picked up from a construction zone in Manhattan. She pushed the strainer over the drain and placed the brick on top. She didn't know if the sight of a liquefied body would bother her, it didn't. The only thing that bothered her was the smell. With the windows open her apartment was cold so she left her coat on and sat in front of her computer. She logged into her profile and wondered if JustFriends would be online. It was probably too early but she wanted to check.

He wasn't online, but had sent her an email. She noticed it had been sent at 4:00am; his nights really were long. She opened the email, and there was only one line. It read "will you be home today, I would like to talk to you about something." She assumed he was going to ask if he could take her to the movies, say after talking with her he thought he was starting to like her, or any other thing a lonely man might say. He wasn't what she was looking for. She thought their next conversation would be their last. She was going to tell him no thanks and block his profile. Yes she replied. She almost felt sorry for him. She had been screwed over in the past and knew how it felt. For a second she wondered if there was a little Beth left her. She thought she'd be nice and tell him she didn't want to meet anyone right now, she was just too busy with work.

She had no intention of letting him come to her apartment, so she replied to his email and said she wasn't sure if she would be home but could they IM later in the day. She asked him to be on his computer around lunchtime and said she could talk then. She would rather tell him she wasn't interested over IM than email so she could be sure he understood. She wanted to end any thought he may have had for a relationship with no concern that he would continue to email her or have hope something more could develop. She found herself surprised at the fact she actually didn't want to hurt him; after all he was a man.

It was Sunday, and in addition to breaking up with "justfriends" she knew she had one important task to complete. She had to get rid of Lotto.

She hadn't been sure what would be left after a night of lye, but after draining the tub, **she** was happy to see how little of him there was. Killing him hadn't bothered her, but she found cleaning him up a little harder. It wasn't the fact he had been a live man the day before, especially since he had tried to rape her, but the disgusting tannish oil-like remains weren't going to be anywhere near as fun as the date. She had never been so happy to have a pair of gloves as she removed what hadn't drained down the tub. She took the small pieces of solid remains on a piece of wood, placed a towel over them, and used her hammer to crush them as much as possible. She poured what was left in a pot and secured it with duct tape. She planned on pouring the remains in the East River, but knew a Sunday afternoon wasn't the best time, so she put the pot in her closet. She wondered if anyone would actually care if they saw her; after all she wasn't in Manhattan anymore.

She sat in front of her computer and thought she would see if Justfriends happen to be online. It wasn't lunchtime, but she had no other plans. He wasn't online, so she started going through the messages she had from potential new dates. Most were the typical, sad just out of a relationship or bored looking for someone fun to meet. She was getting bored herself and was about to sign off when she got an IM from Justfriends. She accepted and realized she wasn't exactly sure what to say. She had ignored and blocked tons of messages, but never talked to anyone long enough to actually have to politely end any communication.

She started typing and was in the middle of saying she wasn't going to be able to meet today and was sorry but didn't think they should when a message popped up. The message simply read, "Not today, but it's important we meet. I'll let you know when I'm coming to see you." Reading this caught her off guard, and she instantly started typing a reply. She said not only were they not going to meet, she didn't want to talk to him anymore, but before she could finish the message he went offline.

33 - GUY FOUR

The fact that he went offline made her angry. Not only had he cut her off, he had taken Morana's control and she didn't like not being in control. The thoughts of what she would say to him the next time he was online were racing through her head when she got an IM from "Youwantme". After the IM with Justfriends, she was livid. Any trace of Beth was gone. Morana was back and Youwantme's profile name made her furious.

She answered the IM without hesitation. She tried to regain her composure when he typed his first IM. His message read "the name says it all". She knew he was next before she started her reply. It took all her willpower to not invite him right over. She took a minute before replying, then asked what he meant. He asked where she was and said she should do herself a favor and meet him. She planned to.

If he wanted to get right to the point, she was more than willing to oblige. Thinking to herself he didn't realize had bad his timing was, she simply replied "why". His message back read every girl does, and you can be next if you're lucky. She replied back, it's your luck you should be worried about. He said he didn't need luck, he had it all, and she would want him just like every other girl. If she hadn't been angry already, the fact that he used the word girl would have been enough to more than provoke her.

She said explain, and he replied all she had to do was look at his profile. She didn't realize until just then she hadn't, so she typed in Youwantme and couldn't help laughing at what popped up. Almost instantly, she knew it was fake. The profile picture looked straight out of GQ and his description read "Gorgeous, huh ladies?" At least he said ladies. He went on to describe himself as the perfect Italian. He said his job was living off his huge inheritance, but that wasn't his only means of satisfying any lady lucky enough to spend the night with him. She thought back to a conversation she had with boring office guy about the box jellyfish and the fact that they had over 60 butts. How nice it would be to feed him to one. Regardless of whether he had a wife, children, or girlfriend, he was next.

Laughing at the fake profile calmed her down enough to regain her composure. She said she was lucky, but with his looks, he had to have a beautiful wife and children who wanted to be just like their dad. He replied they all wanted to be his wife, but he never called any of them back. Smiling to herself, she replied, telling him that after a night with her, she wasn't worried about him calling her back. He said they she should put her theory to the test, and asked when she wanted to meet him. She couldn't help noticing he was blatantly implying she would want to meet him, not the other way around. She wanted to tell him how badly she wanted to meet him this very second and that her theory about him not calling her back wasn't a theory. Refraining she just replied right now. He said see, one look at the profile was all it took. She noticed he said the profile not his profile. Absolutely was all she replied. She couldn't wait and he was right, she wanted him.

She had calmed herself down and was thinking rationally again. She knew she needed to be the one in control so she told him she had to go but hoped he would talk to her again. Always the puppy dog. She said if she was lucky enough to meet him she would have to wear something nice so she needed to do a little shopping. She said she would be gone a few hours but would get right back online so she could talk to him. She asked him what he liked girls to wear and couldn't wait to hear his response. He said a chastity belt was fine but it didn't matter because it was going to be bunched up on the floor as soon as she got him home. He said she should get a big TV because he would was bringing his video recorder incase she liked to watch. She looked at the blue tarp in the reflection of the mirror on her ceiling and replied she loved to watch.

Now calm and with the thought of her hopeful new date she decided she would do a little shopping but not for the kind of things Youwantme had in mind. As she put her coat and gloves on she hoped she would see Chino. He said he was always working but maybe she could talk him into an early lunch break. She wanted to see the look on his face when she told him oxtail was her new favorite food.

34 - THE NOTE

Opening the door she remembered she hadn't turned her computer off. As she turned to go back into the apartment she noticed a note stuck to her door. She stood there perplexed for a moment then her heart started to race. Who would have put a note on her door? Why would anyone have come to her apartment? She thought of the movers but couldn't think of any reason they would have put a note on her door. They only moved one thing and she knew it was where it was suppose to be. She remembered the police had been there and then she started to get nervous. Surely the police would have knocked on the door, they wouldn't have just left a note. It was white notebook paper, wouldn't they have used some official police paper? She looked down her empty hallway and thought it had to have just been a neighbor or maybe the maintenance man saying he would be doing some repair work on her floor.

After looking down the hallway again she felt sure no one was watching her. She slowly removed the note from her door. As she read the note she got shaky and began to feel like she might faint. She closed the door, sat down in her hallway and reread the note. The note simply read "Sorry we couldn't meet today but soon, I'm not just another date", Justfriends.

She sat frozen for a second. She couldn't form a thought without three other thoughts popping into her head. Who knew where she lived, did someone know who she really was, what else could someone know about her... who was Justfriends?

Beth was back and she was scared. She tried to think about what Morana would do but realized the fact that she had to try to think like Morana meant Morana wasn't there. Beth didn't know what to do. Beth wasn't afraid of any suit, large number or the toughest negotiation but she didn't know how to handle the possibility of someone knowing Morana.

She walked to the window and opened it hoping the cold air would help her calm down so she could think rationally. She needed to find out who it was that knew where she lived. She needed to find out what else they knew about her and most importantly she needed to find out where they were.

As the cold air poured into the apartment she could feel her heartbeat slow. She wasn't sweating and didn't feel like she was going to faint every time she stood up. Her fear began to mix with confusion then reasoning. Her fear was subsiding as her resolve to fix this problem began to take over. She could feel a part of Beth being blown away by the cold air coming into through the window. Justfriends had done something no one since Jon had done. Justfriends got Beth's heart racing.

She sat at her kitchen table looking at the reflection in the mirror on Morana's ceiling. She wasn't sure who was looking into the mirror and she wasn't sure who was looking back. Was it the once invincible high stakes no fear Beth or the methodical, no mistakes goddess of death Morana. She knew Beth had crossed and line there was no uncrossing, Morana was the reflection she saw in the mirror.

She wondered if perhaps there was a surveillance camera on her floor but quickly realized she couldn't ask to see it even if there was. She had to be invisible to anyone she didn't want to see her. More calm now she began to think about what her next step needed to be. She had to find Justfriends and fix her problem.

She walked over and opened her

computer. She took a second to try to clear her mind before she logged in. She knew she had say the right thing and more importantly pay attention to anything Justfriends said if he was online. Before she could pull up Justfriend's profile she got an IM from Youwantme, which read no need to shop huh? You decided a chastity belt was enough. Of course he would say the chastity line as a statement not questions. She saw that Justfriends wasn't online and almost shut her computer when she began to wonder if Youwantme and Justfriends were the same people. She realized she was becoming paranoid, it wasn't possible since she had been talking to him when someone put the note on the door. She couldn't help it, she had to fill this guy out just in case.

35 - FINDING FRIENDS

She cautiously asked how he knew she hadn't gone anywhere then realized she had only been offline for a few minutes. She wasn't as clear headed as she thought, Justfriends had her scared and Morana had never been scared. She took a second then said she just wanted to know if he was already spying on her. He said it would be the other way around and she could find out why soon if she was a good girl. That message helped, anger began to drown out fear.

She said she was always a good girl but didn't know anything about him. She asked where he lived and where he thought she lived. She said she knew people lied on their profiles all the time so it was time for him to talk about himself for a while. Rightly so she didn't think that would be a problem. He started right away telling her how the world was his address. He could wake up in Paris and go to bed in Rome. What an idiot she thought, anyone with two hours to kill could do that. She asked if he was in Paris or Rome now and he said who knew, he could be in his private jet on the way to either as they spoke. She asked if his plane ever brought him to the states to which he replied "I told you the world is my address". He was unoriginal as well as an idiot. She really didn't like him.

She let him braggadociously babble about himself for a few more minutes then asked if the world ever let him come to New York. She got so wrapped up in her growing disdain for this guy she almost forgot about the note for a second. While she was waiting on his reply she began to think she was wasting her time, there was no way he was Justfriends. She had much more pressing things to do than to listen to some moron rant about whatever imaginary thing he could come up with at the time. She was about to close her computer and write him off for now when he replied New York was enjoying his company at this very moment.

Her guard instantly flew into high gear. If he was telling the truth could he have put the note on her door. Could he possible be a friend of one of her previous dates that had somehow followed them to her apartment? If so, he could have been talking to her on his cell phone right outside her door. He could have given a bum five bucks to put the note on her door or worse, maybe there was more than one person involved. It was possible. she couldn't take a chance, she had to meet Youwantme.

She started to relax a little at the thought that maybe she was talking to Justfriends and maybe she could find out who he was more easily than expected and most importantly maybe she could fix her problem. She said she was in New York now hoping he would slip up, or maybe even come right out, and say he knew. Instead he babbled a few lines about how good fate was being to her right now and how she might get to see his camera sooner than she had hoped. He was a misogynous idiot and worse one that may know something he shouldn't, she really hated him.

Comforted at the thought that she had found Justfriends she slipped back into calm precise Morana. She wanted to keep him talking. She wanted him to slip up and she wanted to arrange her next date. She said she loved cameras and asked where his was right now. She said she would love to wake up in New York and go to bed watching the snowfall in Australia, she couldn't help **having** some fun with him. She said she was wearing her chastity belt and had her mirror all ready for him. After stroking his ego she waited for his reply. He didn't reply for a minute and she began to wonder if she had called his bluff. Maybe he had to think of a reason he couldn't come see her. She was sure he wasn't some jetsetter, and probably wasn't in New York. He was probably some 15 year old from Idaho in his parent's basement who froze up when a hot girl said he could videotape her.

Her mind started to race again. If he was some 15 year old in Idaho that meant he wasn't Justfriends.

After what seemed like hours he replied. He said he couldn't wait to see her chastity belt and that the snow in Australia was gorgeous this time of year. She didn't care whether he lied about being a world traveler or was just sarcastic, she was glad he was still there. She said that since they couldn't be in Australia at this very moment they should take advantage of all the fun things he could be doing in New York. She said she could show him the sites then show him around New York. She remembered the ridiculous gold chain HungDavid had been wearing and hoped if he was close by he wasn't from Jersey. He said New York was one of his many playgrounds so she could just show him the sites. She hoped he was really in New York. She hoped he was Justfriends. She couldn't get him to her apartment fast enough.

In another attempt to get him to slip us she asked if he knew his way around Manhattan and if so when could they meet. He said he was in Manhattan and they could meet today but she would need time to load up on Red Bull and OJ. What a prick.

It was early Sunday and if fate really were shining down on her an afternoon with Justfriends or Youwantme or whoever he was would be plenty of time. Hoping he wasn't lying she said they could meet for a late lunch at LIC Market where he could watch her chug orange juice. She knew LIC Market was tucked away and close enough to her apartment. She also knew there would be almost no chance they would get a table at brunch without a long wait. If he really was in New York and was anything like the stud he was trying to portray he would be fine foregoing the line, brunch and the orange juice if she were willing to go back to her place. He said he knew where

LIC Market was and he was fine slumming it if that was what she wanted.

Still not convinced he was who he said he was and where he said he was she asked if he wanted to go back to his place. She regretted it instantly. He said he would rather go to his place that way they could eat at a proper place and stay out of the ghetto. She didn't expect him to say that and had to come up with something fast. She said it was fun to slum it every once in awhile and see how the other half lived, besides she had to go to queens anyway. She said she was apartment sitting for her sister while she was away. She was relieved when he offered no opposition, she didn't want to have to continue with any story that would lead to questions. She knew the more she said the more she might have to explain.

If he wasn't lying this was going to be more impromptu than she was used to. She hadn't had time for her always meticulous planning since Youwantme had fallen into her hands so unexpectedly. She wanted to keep it simple.

She asked how she would be able to find him and was surprised when he said his profile picture was real. He said she should just look for the man that stood out in the crowd. Impromptu or not he was going to be fun. She described her every girl looking plain self. Almost worried he might care said she was sorry she didn't get a chance to get all pretty for him. She asked him if he was too handsome to wear a hat that stood out. He said he would wear an orange hat but she would spot the chiseled face before she saw the orange. It couldn't be this easy she thought, fate really had smiled down on her.

36 - YOUWANTME

They arranged to meet at 2:00 and it was already close to 11:00 so she needed to plan and prepare quickly. She knew she would be able to subdue him as long as she could get back to her apartment with no unexpected problems. As she was hiding the stun gun at the bottom of her oversized purse she found herself getting mad. She was getting mad at the fact she had nothing new for Mr. Whoever he was. She didn't care, she was feeling more confident she was about to meet Justfriends and would use a dart gun if that was what it took. He was different, he knew about Morana.

With only two hours to prepare for their date she rushed to organize her "table" and make sure everything she might need was tucked away in the right cabinet or drawer. She made sure to allow herself time to go to the small grocery store one block over. It was a long shot they would have a pineapple this time of year but maybe.

She didn't know what was more miraculous the fact that she had gotten everything in place in two hours or the fact that the store had a pineapple. It was time to meet Justfriends and she was ready

She left her apartment hoping, for the first time she could remember, that Chino wasn't at work. She was relieved when she saw that the man who was always working had apparently taken the day off or was at least eating oxtail, probably with some other snowball. She got into a cab and headed to LIC Market allowing herself plenty of time to get there early as always.

She got the driver to drop her off a block away although she wondered if it was necessary. If it was Justfriends he already knew who she was and where she lived. What actually scared her for a minute was the fact that she didn't know what else he knew about her. She was looking for a stranger, he wasn't. Would he be wearing an orange hat, would he show up was the man she was going to meet even a real person? She didn't care, she was going.

She couldn't' worry about the risk it was a chance she was going to take. She had to take care of her problem.

37 - THE ORANGE HAT

When she saw the orange hat it actually frustrated her that she felt relief instead of her normal intense desire for vengeance. She waited for a second to see if he would come up to her, She wondered if he would call her Beth. Tell her not only did he know what she looked liked he knew who she really was. Only a few feet away, and moving through the line of people waiting on a table, she walked by him. He was certainly aloof If he did know who she was. Realizing after a few minutes that he either didn't know who she was or wasn't going to make contact with her she touched his shoulder. She wanted him to know who she was. She hoped he'd say something that would let her know he was the person she wanted him to be, he didn't.

When he looked at her she realized he was handsome, very handsome. He wore clothes that said money and seemed very well put together. He quietly asked if she was Morana and there was a slight pause before she said yes. For a second she thought she might have made a mistake, thought maybe she should just say no and just but she knew that wasn't an option. He could be playing her but she didn't care, she wasn't going to miss this opportunity. She replied, she was going to take care of her problem.

Youwantme broke the brief silence by asking if he was all she had hoped for or if he was more. For a second she didn't care if he was JustFriends or not, with that comment she was ready to get the date started. She replied he was exactly what she was hoping for. She looked at the long line and said it would obviously be a while did he mind if they made a quick stop by her sister's apartment while the line died down.

Of course he didn't.

They got in a cab and headed back the few blocks to Morana's place. She half laughingly asked if he knew where they were going. He looked genuinely puzzled which caused her a little concern. She said being that he was a jetsetter an all he had to know his way around everywhere. He glanced at her but didn't even break a smile. He really did think he was God's gift to women… and he may have been close. He was they type that even Beth would've hoped would say hello.

The cab pulled up a block over from the back side of her building as usual but again she wondered if it was an unnecessary precaution. If he had put a note on her door, or has she hoped instead, paid a bum to put a note on her door, he already knew where she lived. She had to assume he knew everything about her. She stepped out and said we're here hoping he would say aren't we a block off or isn't that your building or anything that would hint he knew her but again he didn't. All he said was ok, well let's get this started shall we. We definitely shall she said.

As they walked the block, and past an apartment building, he asked where they were going. He asked if that wasn't her building why had the cab dropped them off on that corner. She began to worry that maybe he wasn't being aloof, maybe he really didn't know where they were going, or worse, maybe he didn't know who she was. He had to, it couldn't have been a coincidence she had been IM'ing with Justfriends right as Youwantme came along then Justfriends happened to stick a note to her door. He had to be the right one and she knew how to make him confess.

As she tried to think of an answer to what, at any other time, would be such a simple question she realized how unprepared she was. She couldn't believe it, she couldn't even think of an answer. Was she scared. She said she must have told the driver the wrong address and realized as she was saying it how poor of an answer it was. Of course he asked why she didn't just tell him the right address when he stopped at the wrong block. She said the first thing that came to mind, which luckily happened to stroke his ego. She said she just wanted to show him off but not to worry about it now because they were here.

She rounded the corner of her building and picked up the pace a little so Chino wouldn't see her if he was there. Luckily she didn't see him as she quickly entered her building. Waiting on the elevator she noticed two things, Youwantme's bright orange hat and the fact that she was paranoid as she almost yanked it off his head. He looked at her as if to ask why she was interested in his hat and the doors opened. She gave him a little push and followed him into the elevator. He looked at her pushing the 8th floor button a little too hard and asked if she was ok. Hoping she didn't look as nervous as she suddenly felt she just smiled and said she liked his hair. Just as the door was about to shut someone hurried from around the corner of the lobby into the elevator with them. She had never seen the man in her building but then thought she had probably not seem most of the residents of the building. With a creepy smile he looked at her a little too long. Her mind started racing, did the strange man just need to get to his floor or could her date have arranged for him to be there. Were they working together if so, what did they have planned? She needed to calm down. She asked the guy what floor. He didn't answer her and she couldn't see the button he pushed. For a second she thought about getting out of the elevator but she couldn't, he was in front of her and the doors were closing.

When the elevator started moving she

realized the only button that had been pushed was for the 8th floor. She stared at the back of the stranger's head to see if he acknowledged her date in any manner. The doors opened at the 4th floor and she took a step, she wanted off the elevator but Youwantme grabbed her arm. Looking back at him she felt nervous but he didn't say anything. There was no one waiting for the elevator. The stranger quickly pushed the 8th floor button and the doors shut. She started slowly reaching into her purse for the stun gun when her date pointed at the stranger and shook his head.

After what seemed like hours the doors opened onto her floor and the stranger quickly stepped out then looked back at them. She realized her date was behind her and the stranger was blocking the doors. She felt trapped. She was sure one of the men was Justfriends but who was the other and what were they about to do. Her nervousness was starting to turn panic when the stranger started to speak. He had finished talking before she realized all he said was thanks for the ride then he started walking down the hall opposite the direction of her apartment. She stood there not moving when she felt her date's hand come over her shoulder. She jerked away then realized he was reaching to stop the doors from closing. He looked at her and asked if this was her floor. Still fearful the two were there together she mumbled yes and slowly took a half step out of the elevator. With a puzzled look Youwantme asked if she was lost or if this was her first time. Still uncertain of what to do she forced a smile and started walking towards her door.

About to reach for her keys she realized her date was looking down at her purse. Did he know she had a stun gun and was he waiting for her to pull it out so he could take it from her? Was the stranger going to come back? What was happening? Youwantme looked up at her and asked if she was ok. She could feel herself losing control. She had to pull herself together, she needed to be ready for whatever was about to happen. She turned a little putting herself between her date and her purse then reached in and got her keys. He didn't make any sudden move, he hadn't motioned for anyone to come running around the corner and tackler her. He didn't do anything actually but stand there looking bored.

She unlocked the door and motioned for him to go in. As he stepped into her hall she looked down the corridor once more and saw no one was there. She reached in and pulled her stun gun out of her purse as she stepped into her apartment and turned to shut the door. When she turned back around Youwantme was standing in front of her. He asked her what was going on then took a small step towards her. She wasn't sure if he had seen the stun gun but didn't plan on giving him time to react if he had. She started to bring her arm from behind her back when he turned around and told her to hurry. He said he didn't want to be in this dump any longer than he had to. He said he changed his mind, slumming it wasn't it was all cracked up to be. He was in the middle of telling her he felt sorry for her sister but wanted to go eat then go back to his place when she shoved the stun gun into the back of his neck. He fell instantly. She got the chloroform and zip ties from her bedroom and made sure he wasn't going anywhere.

With her date subdued on the floor and her door now locked she took a deep breath and felt a sense of calm come over her. She had been paranoid for no reason. This wasn't some maniacal master plan, the guy bound in front of her wasn't some evil genius. She had just allowed herself to lose control. That was over now. Morana was back and she had a date.

She realized it was after 2:00 when

saw the clock above the pineapple on her kitchen counter. She rolled her bed into the kitchen and onto the tarp then looked down the hall at Youwantme. He was lean and she knew she could get him onto the bed even without all the adrenaline from the self delusional plot against her. She locked the wheels and maneuvered him onto the bed. As she cut away his clothes she couldn't help thinking about how Beth would cringe at the thought of ruining such an expensive outfit. She duct taped his mouth and eyes then secured each ankle and wrist to the bed railings. She realized she hadn't completely settled down when she saw his right hand starting to turn dark red. She clipped the zip tie and used another one this time trying to be sure it didn't cut off his circulation.

Finally starting to relax, and wait for the chloroform to wear off, she sat in front of her computer and logged in to her profile. It hadn't taken her long to realize this was a great way to vamp up the time she spent with her dates. The more she read through messages from potential dates the angrier she got. The angrier she got the more creative she became. More creativity was never a good thing for the person unlucky enough to be in her bed at the time. She had just started reading through some of her favorites when she heard Youwantme start to mumble.

She walked to the sink and got a glass of cold water to throw on his face to help him wake regain awareness then stood over him watching him slowly come out of his fog. This had become her favorite part of the date. She loved the look in the guy's eyes or watching his heart actually start pumping faster as he began to realize his situation. She liked telling him why he was there and his wrongs that brought him to her bed. But her favorite was watching the jerking and attempts to scream stop as she began to tell them what was about to happen. He quickly became one of her favorites. The others had tried to be macho or threatening but not him. He had manicured nails and perfect eyebrows. He was no macho man, he was terrified. Even covered with duct tape she could see it in his eyes. He didn't try to scream or jerk violently he just lay there paralyzed by fear. She quietly asked him if he knew where he was or who he was with. He didn't move a muscle. She started wishing she had more time and even thought about leaving him there overnight. The terror she knew he was feeling was almost better than anything she was going to do to him, almost.

She decided to leave him to quietly panic a little while longer and walked back to her computer. She had carefully taken his watch off. It was one she didn't recognize and wanted to Google it to see just how much this jetsetter paid to keep time. She was actually shocked when she found it was a Ressence Type 3BB V3 that cost over

40k. She had seen some nice watches on rich men's arms that she knew didn't cost 40k. She couldn't help **having** some fun with him before the date really got started. She walked over to him and could see his body begin to tremble more with each step he heard her take. She leaned over him and said ok, two things. First, how do you value time at this very moment and second, wow, you really are slumming it. She was legitimately trying not to laugh out loud when she heard an IM pop up on her laptop. She laid the watch down on his chest and leaning over his ear quietly said that was a noise he probably didn't want to hear. Walking to her computer, she said to herself, let's see what picture of a penis is going to help kick start my date this time. As she sat down she suddenly filled with a panic equal to that of the man zip tied to her bed.

The IM read "It's time for us to meet. I am downstairs waiting on you...or is this a good time for me to come up"? Your Friend

38 - YOUR FRIEND

She was frozen. There was no way the guy strapped to her bed could have just sent her an IM. Her mind raced back to the guy on the elevator. Did he know? How could he? If they were together in this he wouldn't have let his friend get hit with a stun gun, chloroformed and strapped to a bed without doing something. Maybe he thought his friend was having sex with this hot online girl and their plan was to force her into a threesome. That didn't explain how they knew where she lived. If it had been a friend of one of her other dates certainly they would have reported her when the guy was never heard from again. Was the guy in her bed just some guy who happened to be online at the wrong time. She had no idea what to do but one thing she knew couldn't let happen was someone coming into her apartment. Shaking so bad she could hardly type she responded I'll be down in a few minutes. She looked hopelessly at her laptop screen and Justfriends went offline.

Paralyzed in fear, but knowing she had to go, no one could come up. So many thoughts were racing through her mind. Should she change clothes, put on a different wig, or maybe just jump out of the window? She knew nothing, but perhaps the last idea would help. She tried to steady herself. She looked at her stun gun and threw it into her purse, realizing as she was doing so that it was pointless. She had no idea who she was going to meet but they knew exactly who was coming. She tried in vain to calm down but realized she was trapped. She could only do one thing and that was to go downstairs.

She opened her door and saw no one in her hallway. She walked slowly towards the elevator wondering what went through Youwantme's head when she asked him how he valued time. For her time had both stopped and was racing. She pushed the elevator button and jumped when it opened immediately. Surely whoever was downstairs didn't control the elevator. She didn't realize a person could be this paranoid. She stepped in and pushed the ground floor button. It felt like the doors slammed shut. She hoped it would stop on every floor. She hoped it would fill with so many people it would be a stampede when the doors opened. Maybe just maybe she could stay in the middle of everyone and race through the front door. Even if she did where would she go, what would she do when got there. Someone knew who she was and from that there was no escape.

The elevator hadn't stopped and there was no stampede of people. The door opened on the ground floor and it seemed as if every person was staring at her. Frozen she looked around but didn't see a face she recognized. She was still frozen when she heard a voice asking if she was going back up. She realized there were two people waiting to get into the elevator, she had to get out. She stepped out not knowing what to expect. She wondered if there would be someone standing there holding a sign that read Morana or even worse Beth. No one even seemed to notice her. No one was staring at her other than the two people waiting for her to exit the elevator and they were gone now. She took a breath and started walking through the lobby but nothing looked suspicious. She made it to the middle of the lobby and turned 360 degrees not knowing what to expect but expecting it to be bad. She came to a stop and nothing, no one. She began to wonder what was going on. Who was there, where were they and what did they want? Maybe there was no 10 foot boogie man waiting to grab her. Maybe there was a rational explanation. Maybe someone just saw her online and was nerdy enough to break through all her tech security and just want to meet her. Maybe the boogie man did exist but wanted something else. Maybe he wanted to blackmail her. If he knew she was Beth he knew she had money. Was he even a he? She kept asking herself what was going on, what was she suppose to do. Nothing happened.

She was standing there just like JustFriends asked, but nothing. The longer she stood there the more she realized the only thing happening was that she was in the way. She had stepped out of the elevator, walked to the middle of the room and was now just in everyone's way.

She snapped back to reality when a large woman bumped into her and with a smirk told her to watch where she was going. Watch where she was going, what the hell was the lady thinking? She was standing still and this lady walked right into her. She walked towards the door and started wondering if she would go back upstairs. Had someone wanted to get her out of her apartment. Did someone know what, or who, was up there right now. Maybe someone was freeing Youwantme as she stood there waiting for no one. She had to stop racing through question after question in her head. She had to calm down and try figure out how to handle the situation she had been hurled into. She stepped outside to avoid idly being in everyone's way.

She felt like she could breath once the cold January air filled her lungs. She leaned against her building and for a moment thought about asking a guy a few feet away from her if she could bum on of his cigarettes. Smoking was disgusting to Beth but if it would help her calm down she would smoke every cigarette in queens right then. She pushed herself off the building and started to think about how foolish coming downstairs had been. She walked right out of her apartment with a man tied to her bed who was probably describing her to the police while she was considering taking up smoking. She decided she needed to get back upstairs fast. She stepped forward and reached for the door. Before she could grasp what was happening she heard someone ask if her name was Beth. At the same time she felt someone put a handcuff on her right wrist. She knew the feel of a handcuff.

39 - THE BEGINNING

She was staring into the eyes of a light skinned black man she was certain she had never met. As they were making contact she felt someone forcing her left arm behind her back. She turned and saw a Hispanic guy holding her left arm with one hand while flashing a badge in her face with the other. He began to tell her she had the right to remain silent and the right for something else and so on and so on but it didn't matter. They didn't need to tell her she had the right to be silent, there was no way should could put a coherent sentence together if she tried. She finally managed to ask in a very muffled voice why she was being detained. The Hispanic guy said he would explain everything on the way to the jail. Jail, What was happening and where was Morana? She had abandoned Beth who all the sudden realized she was the person in handcuffs.

The two men rushed her into the back of what appeared to be an undercover police car so quickly the people in front of her building barely had a chance to notice what was happening. In an instance they were in the car and driving away from the safety of her apartment. Forget putting a sentence together, she couldn't put a complete thought together. What did they know, was anyone in her apartment now, would Youwantme starve before he was found. Her mind had never raced so much. She had never been so out of control. She looked at the guy in the passenger's seat and asked why she was being arrested. She tried to explain she hadn't done anything wrong and wanted to know how they knew who she was. Neither man even acknowledged she was asking a question, neither even seemed to even care she was had just been handcuffed and thrown into the back of their car. She started to ask which one of them was Justfriends when she realized neither man had said a word to her other than reading her rights. She stopped in mid sentence just as she started to say Justfriends and the passenger looked back at her like he was hoping she would finish her sentence. Now more questions started running through her mind. Neither man said anything about Justfriends but she almost did. One of them had to be the person who sent the IM otherwise how would they know who she was. What if neither man was Justfriends? If they weren't who were they? Why was she in the backseat of a car with no siren no flashing lights no official looking anything other than two men who were wearing normal clothes.

She was so consumed with questions she didn't notice where they were going. She knew where the local police stations were and she knew they weren't heading in the direction of any of them. They were driving into an area nowhere near a police station. They were driving through back streets and into an area of Queens she knew wasn't safe. Where were they taking her, why wouldn't they talk to her, who were these two men and had she been arrested or abducted? They came to a stop in an alley behind an abandoned building and turned the car off. Neither man said anything, not even to each other. As they sat there parked she noticed a man appear from seemingly nowhere walking towards the car. He was dressed in heavy dark clothing with a hoodie over a hat pulled down almost to his nose. She barely got a chance to see what little of his face that was showing before he go to the car. He leaned into the driver's window just enough to glance back at her. Without saying a word he slipped the driver an envelope and was gone as quickly as he had appeared. She could see the driver take a handful of hundreds out of the envelope and hand them to the passenger who then got out of the car and walked away in the same direction of the guy who gave them the envelope. He asked the driver what was going on, what was he going to do to her but he didn't even glance at her through the rearview mirror. Growing more panicked by the second she asked if he was Justfriends. He turned back towards her and just smiled then got out of the car and walked away. She had no idea what was happening or what to do. She turned her body sideways and tried to open the door but it was locked. She quickly moved to the other side but that door was locked too. She started to push herself up and into the front seat but noticed that even if she had been able to drive the keys weren't in the car. She fell back into the back seat and was trying desperately to think of anything she could do when the guy wearing the hoodie appeared again. He walked to the car, got in the driver's seat and looked back at her. He sat there looking at her for what seemed like an eternity then quietly ask if she would like to meet her friend. As she started to answer he placed a cloth over her mouth. The last thing she remembered was hearing him say this was going to be fun and the car cranking.

She woke sitting upright in a large cloth chair. It took several minutes to regain her clarity then realized she was in a nice room full of expensive fixtures, art and furniture. She wasn't bound in any way and there was no one in the room. She tried to stand but was too groggy. As she fell back into the chair she noticed a letter on the table beside her. It was folded in half and had read quickly written on it in red marker. She grabbed the letter and opened it trying to focus. It read " Beth, you're on the second floor of a hotel and the police are on their way. I would get out quickly. We hope you're as smart as we think you are". JF.

In an instant adrenaline overtook groggy and she started to panic and think at the same time. She heard the sounds of sirens getting closer. She looked over the hotel room and ran towards the door. As she reached for the knob she froze. Was this a setup, who brought her here and what did they mean by as smart as we think you are. The sounds of the sirens were getting closer. She knew she would have to find the answers to her questions later, right now she had to run.

She turned the knob, pushed the door open and flew into the hallway. As she saw the upscale looking hallway half filled with snooty looking people she realized drawing attention to herself was not what she needed to be doing. She tried to pull herself together and walk calmly down the hall. She saw a group of people waiting for the elevator and walked towards them scared to look at anyone. She had no idea where she was and no idea who brought her there. What scared her the most was the note, what did they mean by smart, what did they wasn't from her?

The sirens had been muffled inside the elevator but she quickly realized how close they sounded when the doors opened and she stepped out. She didn't know where she was supposed to go but she knew it was away from the sirens and as fast as possible.

She saw the door, then the first police car and realized calm wasn't a luxury she had time for. She pushed her way through the lobby but when she got to the door she knew that was not a way out. She saw the second and third police car then turned and ran through the lobby. She had no idea how to get out but wasn't going to stay there. For a brief second she wanted to let herself believe they weren't there for her. How did what seemed like an entire police force even know who she was or what she looked like. When the first office entered the lobby she knew that wasn't a chance she could take. She saw an exit sign and started running. She noticed one of the officers pushing his way through the crowded lobby coming her way. She turned the corner towards the hallway with the exit sign and ran as fast as she could. She got to the exit door and almost knocked it off the hinges as she burst out to the side of the hotel.

She saw the flashing lights and started running the opposite direction. She saw lights at the back of the hotel and knew she was trapped. She thought for a second about just giving up. Maybe she should just go back and let them arrest her. Even if she got away what was she going to do and where was she going to go. She didn't recognize her surroundings and her thoughts raced back to the note. JF found her once, and knew she was there. If she escaped the police he was just going to find her again. At least with the police she knew what to expect. She stopped running and as she saw the first office make his way out of the exit a car pulled up beside her. Someone opened the door and she heard him say Morana.

Before she had time to react she jumped into the back of the car and shut the door. Instantly she wondered if she had made a mistake. She expected to hear gunshots and feel broken glass as the police started shooting but nothing happened. The driver didn't say a word he just calmly drove off. As they turned the corner and started driving away from the building her fear turned to confusion. What was going on? It seemed like the entire SWAT team had been chasing her then just decided to let her drive off like nothing ever happened.

She was still trying to figure out what had just happened and why she didn't see a police force chasing them when the driver calmly told her to just relax. He said she was safe and in good hands.

40 - CONFUSION

As they drove down the streets she just sat there stunned trying to see the driver through the dark partition that separated the front and back seats. All the windows were tinted but she could see sunshine and palm trees. She was about to start asking questions when she realized she was in shorts and a t-shirt. She didn't know where she was but she knew she wasn't in New York anymore.

The partition was tinted pitch black, she couldn't even make out a shape of the person driving. Just as she reached out to hit the plastic the partition slowly opened just enough or her to hear a man's voice speak softly and clearly. He said she had been on a trip and she was about to meet Justfriends. He told her to enjoy the ride and raised the partition. She didn't know what to do. She leaned back onto the seat and for a second thought about how much she would give to just be having a painfully boring conversation with the office nerd guy.

The driver didn't say another word, and neither did she, as they drove what seemed to be the longest ride of her life. She noticed they weren't on a highway they were driving down small streets with nice homes and manicured lawns. The longer they drove the more garages each house seemed to have. She felt like they had been driving forever until they pulled into the driveway of what even she would consider a small mansion. When the car came to a stop at the entrance of the house she suddenly realized she didn't want the ride to be over.

She heard the driver open his door. He walked back to her door, opened it and asked her to please come with him. She had to be dreaming, nothing this crazy could actually be happening. She had been abducted, drugged, chased by a Swat team and was now in front of a gigantic house being asked to please follow someone who appeared to be a personal driver.

She got out of the car and followed the man to the door where she was greeted by what appeared to be a maid. She stepped into the house and realized whoever lived there was a person of means. She was escorted into a large foyer where another house servant offered her a drink and asked if she was hungry. More than uncertain of the situation in which she was now in she didn't know what she was suppose to do. She politely said no thank you. The second housekeeper, or whatever employee role she served, asked he to please follow her.

They walked into an opulently designed room where she was asked to please sit anywhere she would like. The cordialness was starting to make her angry. If their plan was too polite her to death it was working. She turned to ask the driver what the hell was going on but he was gone. She sat down.

Both housekeepers walked out and for the second time in several hours she found herself sitting in a chair alone in a room. She had had enough. She didn't care who this person was, she was going to get out of this house and away from where ever she was. As she began to stand she heard a woman's voice. She didn't recognize the person speaking to her but hearing someone speak ended any plan of a great escape.

She couldn't see anyone when the lady began to speak. She began by apologizing for the scene at the hotel. My associate, she explained, reported hearing shots fired. I hoped seeing officers would cause you to flee the building into the safety of my driver's car so we could meet. She went on to apologize for any other inconvenience she may have suffered on her trip and hoped she was comfortable now. She said the manner in which this situation had unfolded was unfortunate but she needed help, the kind of help she was confidant Morana could provide. She could hear the voice coming closer and was shocked when an attractive young woman walked into the room. She said please allow me to introduce myself. My name is Sara but you may know me as Lifesaver.

41 - DECISIONS

Beth didn't know what emotion she was suppose to feel. She was scared because she had basically been kidnapped. She was relieved because she at least knew who was responsible. She was confused because she didn't know what Sara, or Lifesaver, meant be help. She wondered how Sara knew to call her Morana. She wondered if Jon had anything to do with this, if he would be the next person to come from out of nowhere and start talking. She didn't know whether she should politely ask how she could help, try to convince Sara she couldn't help or panic because there was a naked man strapped to a bed in Morana's kitchen.

She had calmed down a bit and was starting to think in a more rational manner, as rational as possible given her situation. She wondered if Sara would actually answer her if she politely asked how she could help. She felt sure explaining how she couldn't help would not work since they hadn't told her what they needed. And she was panicking about the naked man tied to a bed but what could she do about that at the moment, she certainly wasn't going to mention it if they didn't.

Sara began to speak again. She said she believed Beth knew her husband and that he may even be responsible for Morana. She knew they had been in a relationship and she was the person who invited her to the beach. She said I knew you would come and I knew you would see Jon on the beach renewing his vows and I hoped it would keep you away from him. I certainly didn't expect you to react in the way in which you did but I couldn't have asked for a better outcome.

You see Beth, we find ourselves in a mutually beneficial situation. I need Jon dead and I need you to kill him. You need a pot in your closet to be disposed of and something has to be done with the gentleman tied to your bed.

Beth she said, you have a decision to make. You are free to leave, free to go back to Manhattan or queens or wherever you think best given the predicament in which you find yourself. As a way to apologize for the stress we've caused we will even take care of the gentleman with the orange hat. How we resolve that problem is, of course, up to you.

The alternative is you help me with the predicament in which I currently find myself. You see I've been watching you. I have been keeping tabs on you since you decided to sleep with my husband. Actually I have been watching Jon but you became a piece in the puzzle when the two of you began your affair. I watched you, actually I followed you via gps, take you little trip to the mountains. I have visited your storage units and obviously I know where you live. Basically I know more about Morana's activities than you. Isn't technology great.

I don't want you to feel guilty for sleeping with my husband. You see, we all have our little discretions. In fact, I am currently involved in a relationship outside of my marriage. That said, I feel quite certain the purpose for our relationships is different.

You see, this house, these paintings, the driver who brought you here, everything you see belongs to Jon. I don't see the fairness in a husband being able to have affairs, public affairs he doesn't try to hide, while the wife isn't compensated for the shame and embarrassment she suffers. All of Jon's money, the house the company everything is in an LLC which was established before we were married. The one problem with this LLC is the fact that it's safeguarded by an unethical lawyer along with a pre-nup I was mislead into signing.

You see I have spent the last two years working on being given what should rightfully be mine. I would have been fine with a reasonable settlement and an amicable divorce but Jon made sure that would never happen. I could leave but I would leave with nothing. I decided if he felt one person should have everything I should be that person. I am not having an affair but I have been in a relationship. A relationship in which we both share the same goal, the same future the same version of a happy ending.

I have been very busy over these past two years, or should I say we have been very busy. My associate and I have created a sham company. A fictitious company with nothing other than a creatively written piece of software and equally as creative accounting. We show past sales, current sales, future estimated transactions and profits. We definitely show profits, profits and money in the bank, two of Jon's favorite things. It seems there's almost nothing a laptop and printer can't accomplish in today's world. We are so near to seeing you plan to fruition. Jon has gone through our grand creation in detail. He has had his genius team of lawyers, pencil pushers and money chasers dig through our papers and all have found nothing amiss. You see Morana I am as detail, as exact as prepared as you. It seems we have both run into a small but similar problem however.

Our problem is trust. You are here in my home, well Jon's home which I hope you choose to help become my home, but don't no if you can trust me. Of course you aren't certain you can trust me, you don't even know me. I, however, know my partner very well. I know him so well you can thank him for the fact you've found yourself in my humble home. He and I have a very reasonable agreement. We sell Jon our shell of a company which gets his money out of his LLC, out of our pre-nup, and into our hands to be split it evenly. My partner's interest lies abroad so he'll be on the beach of a non extradition country. And me, I'll be the poor cast aside trophy wife who got nothing. Well, nothing except half of Jon's money which will be comfortably housed in an LLC of my own. An LLC whose banking affairs are handled offshore shall we say.

I think my partner has modified his plans recently. As you have discovered I have a knack for keeping tabs on people and I've been keeping tabs on my current little discretion. It seems the closer we get to concluding our transaction the farther away he seems to get from me and the closer he seems to be getting with another young lady. I have noticed in the past that men can tend to be a little greedy and my trust in his intentions is starting to waiver. There is no benefit in my partner's death prior to concluding our business together but there is in a benefit in the death of Jon. I am not entitled to anything in the event of a divorce but I get it all should my beloved husband suffer and untimely demise.

Here is where you come in Morana. Your problem is you leave dead men lying around. My problem is I need one of those dead men to be my husband. You remember my husband, the man who broke your heart and from what I can see created the very person you've become. It appears he is the foundation of all your problems so who better to exact revenge.

Now back to the gentleman tied to your bed. The associates that help me keep watch over people who need to be watched are quite handy at doing other jobs, the type of jobs few people are qualified to do. Not only are they qualified they are very good, very resourceful and very efficient. They truly are an indispensable asset. These associates can be very beneficial to a person who finds themselves in need. As I see it there are several people in need at the moment. I have just explained my need, I think we are all beginning to understand the need you have and it would certainly be remiss of me to overlook the need of the gentleman in your kitchen. It seems it would bode well for both of us to form a partnership of sorts. You help me get rid of a man and I will help you get rid of a man. In fact I will remove three unwanted men from your life.

So Beth, what is Morana's answer. Do we each take care of the others problem or do my friends help the gentleman in your kitchen avoid what I am sure would have been a very agonizing death. I can see the look on the detective's faces as they sit on the edge of their seats listening to every word the orange hat has to say. Beth you should be proud, Morana is so accomplished I don't think the most polished detective would believe him at first. Surely he's making up such an outrageous story. A woman strapping grown men to a bed against their will, then using a torture table to inflict unimaginable pain before ultimately killing them. That couldn't be true, they would need more proof. The kind of proof her friends could ensure was never found. In fact, her friends could ensure the orange hat never has the opportunity to have that little chat with that polished detective. The one so polished he wouldn't stop until the case was solved and the guilty party was brought to justice.

All Beth could think about was why she called it a torture table. It couldn't have been a coincidence that she just randomly said torture table. She couldn't remember, had she used those words on the guy in her kitchen. Even if she had there was no way he could have told Sara that was what she called her date tray. How did she know that, how did she seem to know everything? Who the hell was this lady and how could Morana get rid of her? That was the real question and she was going to play along until she could find the answer. Morana was back, fear and Beth were fading. I am happy to take care of your problem Morana replied.

42 - EXPLANATIONS

Morana wanted to put Sara at ease, she wanted to be believed. She painted on a smile, sat down and acted as calm as she could. She asked if she could still have that drink and said they she wanted to know more about Sara in her least threatening voice. Light heartedly she said it didn't seemed fair Sara knew all about her while remaining such a mystery. It appeared to work, Sara asked for a drink too and asked if vodka on the rocks would work then gave instruction for drinks to be brought to them. She came closer and sat in the chair closest to Beth then asked what Morana would like to know.

With the tension easing she asked Sara how she had been able to create such an elaborate scheme and make the shell of a company so believable and why she couldn't just have her associates take care of her Jon problem. She asked how she found out about her and Jon and explained she had no idea he was married. She asked Sara how she had been able to find out so much about Morana and why vodka. Sara smiled.

Sitting back in her chair Sara said let's start from the beginning. She said I wasn't interested in Morana at first, she was just another of Jon's girlfriends that had been discovered while he was being watched, She said at first my plan was to do simply gather proof of the affair then bring you to the beach for the purpose of getting you out of the way. I hoped you seeing us renew our vows would be enough for you to end the relationship. She said I make it made it common practice to continue to watch Jon's girlfriends for a while to be sure they aren't going to cause any problems, just long enough to be sure they end the affair and stay out of the picture. She said I was about to stop having you followed until you rolled a guy to your car in a wheelchair. She said that sparked my interest so I decided to have one of my associates find out a little more about you starting with why you were with a guy in a wheelchair and where you were going. She said I was simply curious until I found out you made a trip to West Virginia with your friend then came home by yourself.

As for the fake company she said that was a long boring story they could discuss in the future and having one of her associates do her dirty work wasn't as safe as having a stranger take care of her problem. She said you just never know who you can trust. Even someone close to you like a wife might turn on you if there is a financial benefit to be gained. Besides, given how I can help you it is less likely you would try to try to implicate me should any legal problem arise. After all, it would be much easier to deal with one issue than adding the explanation of a trunk in a storage unit that shouldn't be there. Jon's pre-nup taught me a valuable lesson in always covering yourself she said. I regret having to put you in this position but not knowing how I help you with your problems should keep me safe should you run into a little problem with a police officer while helping me with mine.

As for finding out about Morana, you made that easy. Trying so hard to remain unseen Morana kept herself in her own little prison of sorts. You rarely ventured outside of your apartment and even then it was a short trip to get an important item or to meet a date only to race him back to your bed. You remained secluded in your own small bubble over the weekends and were gone all week. Finding you was never a problem and knowing what you were doing and when you planned on doing it became easier the first time you left your laptop unattended. Technology these days is amazing wouldn't you agree. We simply downloaded an untraceable program onto your computer that allowed us to see the sites you visited, provided us with your login information and basically anything else you did on the internet. You did a commendable job on keeping your movement secure right down to building an almost impenetrable firewall around the technology you used.

You are smart, very smart, which is another reason you are here. You were smart in the manner in which you used phones, the library and secure internet connections. The one area of surveillance you overlooked was right in front of you. You didn't take a single precaution to protect the camera in your laptop. Once we were able to see you, to watch you work, things became easy for us. We know as much about Morana as Beth does, maybe more. We know how to get rid of those little loose ends Morana has yet to tie up.

As for vodka, it doesn't stain your teeth. Beth couldn't help smiling.

Now let's talk about our more pressing problems Sara said. I believe it is safe to say you have someone in your kitchen you would rather not be there. You also have someone in a chest you would like to be rid of and a rather grotesque pot in your closet filled with an implicating little broth that has yet to be thrown out. These are things I am happy to ensure are never uncovered. They are also problems, that given the chance, you could remedy yourself. You could also dispose of your tray and all of its nasty little contents, make sure Morana's apartment is clean, disinfected and free from even the slightest trace of DNA. After that you could pay the remaining lease in full, move out of the slumps back into Beth's posh carefree lifestyle. For Beth however, a few problems remain that aren't quite as easy to be rid of. You used the internet, which is an indispensable necessity with one major flaw. Once information finds its way onto the internet if becomes trapped with no way off. Those little pieces of information live on in perpetuity. You also made several other small mistakes you didn't realize you were making like leaving fingerprints that have already been copied and talking to an inexpensive lucky little guy at your storage safe house. There are more but I think my point had been made.

That said, I meant it when I said Morana is very accomplished. Left unencumbered I she may have been able to continue with her work until she simply decided to retire. I'm so impressed with you I think we can dispense of any threatening conversation from this point on. I think you might actually enjoy, perhaps even want to help me with my little favor. Morana is a planner not to different from myself. I have seen how careful how meticulous you are and although the transaction I am close to completing hasn't been fully explained I feel you can respect how detailed it must have been to accomplish. Simply put, and at the risk of sounding redundant, I need your smarts and you can benefit from the smarts of my associates. If you don't find yourself too exhausted from your trip what's say we have another stain free vodka and talk shop?

It was Morana's turn to talk again but she was beginning to realize her lack of options. She thought about playing nice until the opportunity to find a bed to strap Sara in presented itself but knew that wasn't realistic. Even if she were able to get Sara out of her life she had no idea who her associates were, what they knew and most importantly what they might do. She found herself in a position in which she had no contention plan, she found herself not only with no control but being controlled. She was at the mercy of Lifesaver.

43 - THE PLAN

She knew the one choice she had was the only choice she had been given. For a moment she thought it would be nice to exact revenge on Jon. She thought how nice it would be to make him pay for breaking her heart, for creating Morana and for the pain he had cause any girl in his life whom he had treated like he treated Beth. As angry as she was at the situation she was being forced into she almost felt Sara deserved revenge for the way he treated her. Sara's had planned a different type of revenge, her plan was to take what she felt she had earned. She wouldn't allow herself to pity Sara. Maybe a big house, nice cars and fancy artwork were all she hoped to gain from the relationship. Maybe she had never loved Jon.

After the second round of vodka tonics were delivered and the maid had been excused she asked Sara what she needed her to do. She said she understood the expected outcome but what was the plan. Sara told her it had all been mapped out. The way in which she and Morana were going to solve her problem would be simple and would allow both of them to resume their lives without fear of retribution. She had all the details worked out and all Morana had to do was follow them. She wondered where all of Sara's prim and proper went once the conversation turned to a more frank discussion about how she wanted her husband killed. She wondered what ulterior motives Sara had. She wondered if she was actually going to have to do this.

The more Sara spoke the more Morana began to hope this had been planned with precision and detail. She asked Sara why she had waited until this exact moment to bring her into the plot. She expected some complicated extended answer about how the timing had to be just right. How Jon was going to be in a certain place at a certain time or that they only had one chance. Sara simply replied she needed him dead before it was too late.

The answer wasn't what she expected, and after hearing it she knew it wasn't the answer she'd hoped for. She would have been more at ease if Sara had explained in detail some elaborate plan involving an exact time and location with a precise escape plan or way out if things didn't go just right. She had done this before and she knew you couldn't plan for "because it needed to be done before it was too late". She started to worry.

44- INTRODUCTIONS AND DECEPTIONS

Sara stopped talking in a manner almost as unexpected as she had started. It took Beth a minute to realize a third servant had silently walked into the room. Sara looked at the servant, who simply nodded her head then walked away. With a smile, Sara looked back at Beth and said, "It's time to take care of our little Jon problem. Looking at Beth, Sara motioned towards the side entrance of the room and said she had some friends she would like Morana to meet. "These are some friends who will help you with any need you may have or any issue that may arise this evening," she said.

"Oh, by the way," she said. "You're going to kill Jon tonight.

Beth had only taken a few steps when two men walked into the room. She was caught off guard. She didn't know their intentions. Were they going to attempt to hurt her and, if so, how could she protect herself? Were they the people Sara said would help her with any issue...the Jon issue? She had been so focused on the two men she didn't notice Sara leave the room.

The men were intimidating. They were both in shape, well dressed, and appeared intense and very serious. The first was short, had dark hair, and looked like he spent every possible moment in the weight room. The second was tall and lean and seemed to be the person who would be giving instructions. He sp**oke, and I**t quickly became all too apparent they weren't there to help or assist her, they were there to ensure Morana did exactly what she was told.

In a polite but very direct manner, he asked her to please follow him. Why the 'please' she wondered? He wasn't giving her the option to say no. Why not just say "Follow me" or even more accurately, "Follow me or I will make you follow me?" What did he think manners would accomplish? Did he think saying pretty please before giving her a gun and telling her to kill someone would make everything ok? What could she do, she followed him through a hallway and out a door that exited to the side of the house.

She saw a black limousine with windows so tinted you couldn't see in the car. Her mind, her heart, and her adrenaline all began racing at once. Where was the car going to take her this time? She felt confident it wasn't going to be a gorgeous house with artwork, servants and stain free vodka. She felt a hand on her back as her step slowed. The short meathead was helping her involuntarily continue move towards the car as the one in charge began to explain the agenda. He said his associate would accompany her to be sure there were no problems and the gentleman driving would provide her with instructions. Very to the point, he explained both men were there to provide her support by any means necessary in the event she began to question her ability to follow through with her job.

Meat head opened the door, and with his hands still on her back, assisted her in the back of the limo. He got in behind her and shut the door. When the door shut, the sunlight disappeared. It was so dark and so quiet. She couldn't see outside she couldn't hear outside. The interior of the car seemed void of everything except fear, she was afraid.

It seemed the sound of the door being

closed had just left her ears when she noticed the partition begin to lower. As it slowly came down, she saw what appeared to be a silencer, then a barrel and finally the grip. As the partition fully opened a man's hand appeared, a hand that was pointing a gun at her. Before her terror could turn to panic, the man fired the gun. She thought she had to be dead, being shot had to be excruciating, but she felt no pain. With the interior of the car enveloped by the smell of gunpowder, she slowly opened her eyes. She saw blood on her, but quickly realized it was from Meathead. Even through the smoke, she could see the hole in his forehead. Frozen and overwhelmed by her situation, she heard a voice begin to speak. It was a man speaking and she sat quietly as he said "She is going to kill you after you kill Jon." The man's face appeared from behind the partition and looking at her he said "I told you. I'm always working, Snowball."